THE DESTROYERS OF LAN-KERN

... a strange w___ ___ ___ of _ll_ ___ ___ ___ out all other ___ ___ nesting in nea___ alarm and bi___ the undergr___ nothing Kig___ rhythmic, cou___ tify it with no___ stood rooted to the spot gazing with startled eyes, trying to locate the source of the sound.

It was above her.

Suddenly a large black shadow fell between her and the serene white light of the moon.

She looked upwards and screamed in terror.

By the same author

THE FIRES OF LAN-KERN

PETER TREMAYNE

The Destroyers of Lan-Kern

Methuen

A Methuen Paperback

THE DESTROYERS OF LAN-KERN
ISBN 0 413 50730 0

First published in Great Britain 1982
by Methuen London Ltd

Copyright © 1982 by Peter Tremayne

This edition published 1983
by Methuen London Ltd
11 New Fetter Lane, London EC4P 4EE

Printed and bound in Great Britain by
Cox & Wyman Ltd, Reading

This book is sold subject to the condition that it shall not, by
way of trade or otherwise, be lent, resold, hired out, or otherwise
circulated without the publisher's prior consent in any form of
binding or cover other than that in which it is published and without
a similar condition including this condition being imposed on the
subsequent purchaser.

This second excursion into the world of

Lan-Kern is for my niece

DARA GALIĆ

with love.

PART ONE

The Land of the See-ti

"The hero, he who is without fear and righteous in the cause of justice; the wise man; the true friend and the compassionate adviser, is sought everywhere but only found in fragments. Therefore is the same true of the tyrant, the coward, the foolish man, he who is weak and untrustworthy and is inconsiderate or despotic. There never was, and never can be, a hero who is faultless, a wise man who is not foolish nor a compassionate man without a trace of intolerance. Neither can there be an evil person who has not a corner for goodness and love in his heart. There is no such thing as perfect good nor perfect evil. There are only the complexities of human reactions."

An Lyver Mur a Lan-Kern
The Great Book of Lan-Kern.

CHAPTER ONE

The great forest was dark and threatening. Tall conifers, interspersed with squat and gnarled trees and countless shrubs and bushes, stretched up to the distant night sky, almost blotting out its vista from the ground. The thick undergrowth constantly rustled and whispered in the faint breeze or at the sudden passage of some nocturnal creature. The brooding blackness was unfriendly, fraught with unidentifiable dangers.

The girl paused in mid-stride, head to one side, cautiously listening to the constant night noises. She could separate some of the noises - the hoot of an owl, the croaking and erratic choir of frogs and the shrill chirping of crickets. She peered around, her pale, heart-shaped face stretched in a mask of anxiety. Her delicate lips were compressed into a thin line showing white at the corners of her mouth. Her knuckles also showed white where her slender hand gripped a short javelin.

Kigva, daughter of Kesmur, high chieftain of all the tribes of Lan-Kern, had long since given herself up as being lost - hopelessly lost. When she had fled from the great fortress of Nelferch-an-Gwargh, the tyrannical witch queen of Lan-Howlek, Kigva had believed she was escaping westward, back to the safety of Lan-Kern. But she had not considered the devious and twisting path of the tunnel through which she had fled from the fortress; a path which had caused her to lose her sense of direction. So sure of her direction had she been that she had not paused when she emerged from the earthy burrow into the midst of the thick forests but had pressed on immediately, away from the fortress of Dynas Drok - the Fortress of Evil; away as swiftly as she could until sheer exhaustion finally forced her to stop and curl up by the bole of a tree to rest. She had fallen asleep immediately and only opened her eyes when the fierce light of day managed to filter through the tightly overlaid branches. In that sleep of exhaustion she had missed the tell-tale advent of dawn which would have indicated that she was going in the wrong direction.

Kigva had stood up perplexed and examined the green gloom of the daytime forest. She had been worried because she had not already reached the great river which marked the boundary of Lan-Kern and Lan-Howlek and even at that stage it had crossed her mind that she had gone in the wrong direction. It was impossible to see the position of the sun through the foliage. She found some fruit, ate sparsely, and drank from a nearby stream. Then she pressed onward hoping to find a clearing in the forest where she could obtain a look at the sky to find her directions. But for most of that day she had continued through the unfamiliar terrain, finding no open space among the densely growing trees. The journey itself was easy for there were no signs of the larger wild creatures, creatures such as the terrifying *gourgath,* which were said to inhabit these forests. Indeed, she saw no animal larger than a wild dog which, at her scent, paused and then turned swiftly away into the protection of the denser undergrowth.

It was late in the day when she paused again, this time with a feeling of despair rising within her. It was now obvious to her that she was lost and was not heading westward towards Lan-Kern. Her mind began to allow wild thoughts to emerge into her consciousness. She began to have an inexplicable fear that she was being followed. The feeling of eyes watching her from the undergrowth, following her progress, sending shivers down her spine, became strong. Was she being pursued by the warriors of Lan-Howlek? Cador, Nelferch's arrogant and despotic grandson, would certainly follow her to exact revenge. As soon as the hopeless slave rebellion, under cover of which Kigva had contrived her escape, was crushed, it was inevitable that Cador would begin his pursuit of her.

She shuddered and peered in bewilderment along the path she was following. If she was not heading westward to the safety of Lan-Kern perhaps she had wandered eastwards? Kigva had heard many weird legends throughout her young life about the land that was supposed to lie to the east of Lan-Howlek - the land that the ancients had called the See-ti. Legend had it that it was a strange, terrifying country peopled by werefolk, people who might be gods from the

Otherworld, people who could shoot lightning bolts at their enemies and oft-times flew in the bowels of great birds. But of the various expeditions of warriors which ventured into the eastern lands to discover the veracity of the legends, not one had returned.

Kigva shuddered again. Was she unwittingly travelling into that terrifying country - the land of the See-ti? With a sense of desperation she pressed on, every nerve sensitive to sound, however insignificant.

Night had suddenly embraced the forest again in its black forbidding shroud and still Kigva had been unable to discover a clearing from which to examine the sky and get her bearings. She had almost given up this plan when she saw it; a shaft of brilliant moonlight bathing a large open space before her, lighting it almost as bright as day.

With a stifled cry of joy she ran forward. The clearing was large and seemed to be a small plain of tall but flopping grass. Kigva, her heart beating gladly, ran forward to the centre of the plain and stood staring up. Her eyes, trained by old Melyon the female *drewyth* of Pen-an-Wlas, sought out the familiar lights in the sky. To Kigva the sky was as readable as a map. It confirmed her fears. For the past two nights and a day she had been moving eastwards. She cursed softly. But, above all, Kigva was a practical girl. She did not waste any words of recrimination on herself but stood swiftly picking out an intended path westward from the night sky.

It was then that a strange whirling sound filled the air, drowning out all other noises of the night, causing the birds, nesting in nearby trees, to flap skyward in sudden alarm and bigger animals to go crashing through the undergrowth in terror. The noise was like nothing Kigva had ever heard before. It was a rhythmic, coughing type of sound. She could identify it with no animal she had encountered. The girl stood rooted to the spot gazing with startled eyes, trying to locate the source of the sound.

It was above her.

Suddenly a large black shadow fell between her and the serene white light of the moon.

She looked upwards and screamed in terror.

Cador, grandson of Nelferch of Lan-Howlek, paused for a rest beside a small gushing stream and lowered to the ground before him the black metal box which he had been carrying on his shoulder. Then he unbuckled his sword belt and laid his weapons on the bank before kneeling to scoop up a handful of the cold, crystal water. He wiped his mouth on the back of his hand and peered round. His black eyes caught something on the ground near him and a smile etched his sallow face.

In spite of an indolent and self-indulgent childhood and youth, Cador had learnt the art of woodcraft well and had been following Kigva's trail without difficulty. But it needed no trained eye to see the broken grass by the bank of the stream nor the indentations in the mud where the girl had obviously knelt to drink.

He reached forward and ran a finger gently around the edge of the indentations made by the girl's knees. The mud was still soft, and the marks therefore were not old - an hour or two at the most. He had made good time in spite of being hampered by the necessity of carrying the black box.

He bent back to the stream and splashed his face and neck with the water then sat back. Since the slave rebels, led by the *estrennek*, the foreigner called Dryden, whom the men of Lan-Kern had named Yaghus - the healer, had broken into his grandmother's fortress, Cador had not known a moment's peace nor rest. Now he closed his red rimmed eyes and allowed himself the luxury of a nap. Even asleep his mind was active with memories, reliving the moments when the risen slave rabble had burst into Dynas Drok and overthrown his grandmother. He had heard she had been slain and Bel the Creator alone knew what had happened to his mother Logosen. Not that he felt any anxiety nor remorse for he hated both Nelferch and Logosen.

Cador had been raised by his mother and grandmother at Dynas Drok. Nelferch's ambition for power had ruled everything with a single-minded purpose that caused all other emotions to be subservient to it. That driving ambition had probably been the cause of the instability of Logosen's mind. As a mother she had been quick tempered, foul-mouthed, and to Cador's recollection she had never spoken one word of endearment to him nor even touched him as a mother might touch her son. Cador's father had died shortly before he was born but even had he lived he would have hardly

6

protected Cador for he was a weak man. As it was Cador grew to manhood with a sullen resentment and deepset hatred of Nelferch and Logosen and this was reflected in his contempt for all women and a suspicious hatred of people in general.

Cador was not a coward nor a bully by nature but the environment of his childhood had inevitably produced in him the urges for self-preservation and self-gratification to the detriment of all other considerations. Therefore, when Cador realised that the slave rebellion led by Dryden was on the verge of success, that Nelferch had been slain, he had fled through the secret passage which linked his chambers to the eastern forests. As he fled he had taken the black box - *An Kevryn,* The Mystery - the *drewyth* symbol of the meaning of life and the universe; the sacred relic which he and his warriors had plundered from the great *drewyth* sanctuary of Meneghy in Lan-Kern. According to the *drewyth* teachings, no man should look into the black box to discover the secret of life lest he destroy the place and purpose of man in the creation.

Cador stirred uneasily. Before the *estrennek* Dryden had led the slaves of Lan-Howlek in revolt, Cador had two prizes: *An Kevryn* and the beautiful daughter of Kesmur, Kigva of Lan-Kern. She had been taken in a slave raid at the time when Cador plundered Meneghy. Kigva had been a pretty prize indeed - and daughter of the high chieftain of Lan-Kern! An alliance there could have furthered Cador's own plans to overthrow his grandmother. But his soul blazed in black rage as he recalled Kigva's rejection of him. He had with great magnanimity, as captor to captive, offered the girl marriage and she had spurned him. Spurned *him!* Never in his life had anyone dared to deny him that which he wanted.

And when the slaves had risen and he had been forced to leave his chambers to take command of the guards, Kigva had discovered his secret passage and fled into the forests. Returning, and seeing all was lost, Cador had seized *An Kevryn* and hurried after her, following her escape route away from the conquering rebel-slaves. He had no plan at first other than to put distance between Dryden and the victorious slaves and himself. But as he followed the fleeing girl a plan formed in his mind. With *An Kevryn* and Kigva of Lan-Kern in his possession, Cador might be able to strike a bargain with the new rulers of Lan-Howlek.

He opened his eyes and stared down at the black box by his side.

'The Mystery, eh?' he whispered as his hand almost caressed its cold metal exterior. 'There is no mystery to the power you hold. You have power enough to buy my life and freedom from the vermin that now rule Dynas Drok. If you truly hold the secret of creation then no hand but mine shall open you.'

He spent a futile period trying to prise open the box, banging at it with a stone, but the complicated locks, which no *drewyth* had been able to figure in hundreds of years, remained closed. Cador gave up the attempt in disgust.

Now he glanced up at the onset of the evening gloom and decided that he must continue his pursuit of Kigva. The trouble was that the box would slow his progress. It would be better to bury it and return later. Buckling on his weapons again, he raised the box on his shoulder and struck off along the bank of the stream, following the tracks left by the girl in her hasty flight. He would bury the box at the first suitable spot he found.

It was about an hour later when he came across such a spot. It was a small half-obscured cave mouth set a little way back from the river. He put the box down and forced his way to the cave and sniffed suspiciously. Had it been the lair of some animal he would have smelt traces of the beast but, apart from the tangy smell of confined earth and a slight dampness, there was no sign to indicate occupation of the cave.

Reassured, he set to digging hastily with his knife - scraping rapidly at the soft earth. It was fairly easy work and soon he had uncovered a hole large enough to take *An Kevryn*. Piling the earth over it was an even easier task. Then he withdrew from the cave and, with quick, nervous glances, began to arrange the foliage and shrubs to disguise the fact that they had been disturbed. To a casual onlooker the undergrowth would now show no impression of disturbance. Using a broken branch, Cador brushed away all traces of footprints as far as the bank of the stream. He stood for a moment taking careful note of the position of the cave and then turned and moved eastwards, following Kigva's tracks.

As Cador passed out of sight through the forest a patch of undergrowth on the far side of the stream directly across from the cave trembled and was pushed aside to reveal a tall, burly giant of a man. He was heavy of frame with a coarse black beard, a scarred face and small black eyes.

The man stood for a moment, listening. He was dressed in garish clothes and a large double-edged sword hung low on his hip. His tiny, glinting eyes looked for a long time in the direction in which Cador had disappeared. A frown creased the man's face as he looked towards the hidden cave mouth. Then gradually a grin split his thick lips, showing uneven and blackened teeth, and with a sudden grunt the giant splashed through the shallow stream towards the cave.

CHAPTER TWO

It was dawn when Cador followed Kigva's trail into the forest clearing and stopped in bewilderment. He gazed at the ground where his trained eye could see her tracks plainly; see the trampled, broken grass and the indentations in the soft earth - all the marks which a skilled tracker could read as plainly as the texts written by the *drewyth*. It was evident that the girl had entered the clearing and stood in its centre awhile, and then - then it seemed as if she had vanished, for the tracks ceased abruptly. They did not continue nor were they retraced to the forest.

Cador frowned. Around the spot where the tracks ended the grass was blown this way and that as if by strong contrary winds. And what was this? He dropped to one knee and examined some small patches of burnt grass. He had seen forest fires before and knew their signs, but these were strangely different. The grass appeared to be singed at its tips with the roots barely touched. This was mysterious.

Legends of the land of the See-ti came unbidden to his mind; legends recounted by old, wizen-faced men in their cups. Nonsense! Men who could shoot lightning bolts and fly in the bowels of great birds - surely these were fairy tales for children? Tales to coax the disobedient into dutifulness?

A scream, long and drawn out, caused him to leap to his feet. It was the scream of a woman. He stood still for a moment, head to one side, weapons clutched firmly in his hand, waiting for the scream to come again and tell him the direction.

It came; strong and vibrant. Cador set off at a quick trot through the forest towards the sound. A little further on the forest gave way again to an even bigger clearing, severed by a twisting stream. Cador pulled back into the safety of the bushes and dropped to a crouching position. Standing in the clearing were a group of a dozen men who were in the process of breaking camp, some folding rough made tents of animal skins and another dousing a fire with water from the stream. They were all armed with broadswords and bows and arrows; all were dressed in brightly coloured costumes. And in their midst was a young girl.

Cador's eyes narrowed. Not for a moment had he doubted that it was Kigva. But as he examined her his mouth drooped in disappointment. The girl had long ash-blonde hair and while she was attractive she was certainly not the daughter of Kesmur of Lan-Kern. Cador saw that her arms were tied behind her back and that one of the men, a grey bearded giant, was leering at the girl as he towered over her. Cador strained forward. The men were talking in a language that was strange to him but the girl was now berating the giant in the *Kernewek*, the language common to Lan-Kern and Lan-Howlek.

'If you strike me again, vermin, I shall do more than scream,' she cried, tossing her long hair away from her face and staring defiantly at the man.

The grey bearded giant roared:

'I am much frightened by your threat, little maid.' He spoke in the same language but stumbling and with a heavy accent. He held out his hands in mimicry of a supplicant. 'Please do not harm me.'

He turned and rapped out something to the men nearby and they joined in his coarse laughter.

Cador felt a moment of admiration for the girl standing there, bound as she was, yet defying these giants. From her speech she was obviously a maid of Lan-Howlek. Why had they taken her prisoner? Who were they? Surely these were not the mythical warriors of the See-ti?

The grey bearded giant was speaking to the girl again.

'We will teach you respect, little maid, when we bring you safe to our ship.'

'You will teach me nothing, *morlader*,' retorted the girl.

Realisation dawned in Cador's mind. *Morlader*! These were pirates and buccaneers from the northern lands who often frequented the coasts of Lan-Howlek and Lan-Kern, raiding and plundering unprotected ships and coastal settlements. He had never seen them before though he had met many people who had witnessed their

11

vicious raids. No, these were certainly not the mythical demi-gods of the See-ti, these were flesh and blood men such as himself. But why were they so far inland? Obviously they were on some raid, but where did their ship lie? Had they already taken Kigva prisoner? It seemed likely. If only he could speak to the girl captive, she might be able to help him. Cador bit his lip in thought. No, there was certainly no question of him attempting a rescue against a dozen of these bearded barbarians.

He watched from his cover as they finished breaking camp and packing their bundles. The grey bearded man seemed to be their captain and Cador heard the others respectfully address him as Beoc. He turned his attention again to their captive. He judged her to be about twenty years old. She was watching the proceedings with a haughty indifference on her finely chiselled features. There was no fear nor alarm on her face and once again Cador felt a small thrill of admiration.

Now he noticed that the man, Beoc, was standing with his hands on his hips looking towards the jungle. There was a worried look on his features causing his eyebrows to knit across the bridge of his nose in concern. Then he raised his voice.

'Conla! Conla!'

He waited as if for an answer. It did not take Cador long to realise that the man was calling for one of the band who had gone off into the forest. One of the other men turned to Beoc and said something, shaking his head and pointing to the sky. At this the girl laughed.

'He will not come back to you, *morlader*,' she sneered. 'The gods of the See-ti have him by now.'

The giant turned to her with a scowl.

'Shut up, wench!' he snapped in his guttural accent. 'Conla will return soon.'

'Oh?' smiled the girl. 'And who was it, then, that was carried off screaming into the air by the giant bird last night? Did we not hear the bird hovering? Did we not hear the scream as it pounced upon its prey over there?'

Cador saw the girl incline her head in his direction and with a sudden coldness realised that she was indicating the clearing into which he had followed the tracks of Kigva - the tracks which had abruptly disappeared in the middle of the clearing *as if she had*

12

vanished into the air. A vague feeling of fear came upon him and he glanced skyward. Could it be that Kĭgva had been seized by - by what? Surely the legends about the See-ti could not be true?

The grey bearded giant was speaking.

'We *morlader* do not hold with your fairy tales of gods and ...'

'Then why did you hide in your tents last night when we heard the sounds of the great bird?' interrupted the girl with a bitter laugh. 'And where is your warrior who went into the woods yesterday ... the man with the black beard? Answer me that, *morlader*?'

The man stared at her for a moment, opened his mouth to speak and then turned his back on her. He muttered something to the others and they shouldered their packs. The man, Beoc, passed a rope around the girl's neck and holding the end of the rope in one hand he started across the clearing.

It all happened so suddenly that Cador had no time to think. It was like some vision from a nightmare over which he had no control.

As the *morlader* set off there came a sudden sound, a strange whirling noise, a rhythmic coughing like nothing he had heard before. It was loud, so loud that he wanted to hold his hands over his ears. Above the tree tops on the far side of the clearing a black object rose into the sky and hung there for a moment blotting out the sun. Cador stared at it aghast, scarcely believing his eyes.

It had a black bulbous body which tapered to a thin tail at one end. It seemed to have two large colourless eyes above which something whirled with a frenzy, moving faster than the wings of a bee. It was larger than any flying animal that Cador had seen before. But what was horrific - really horrific - was that Cador could clearly see a human face peering out from within the eye, while in a gap just behind the eye another human shape was balanced, pointing a short black stick down towards the *morlader.*

The *morlader* had frozen, gazing up in apparent disbelief at the terrible apparition which now rose above the trees and then swept down into the clearing before them. Beoc moved first, letting loose the rope by which he had led the girl captive, fumbling with his broadsword and cursing and shouting at the others. The men broke into action and several fled towards the trees. Two, braver than the rest, strung their bows and loosed several arrows at the creature.

One arrow, Cador saw it well, actually struck the creature on the eye and, to his amazement, bounced harmlessly off. Then something even more incredible happened. The human form standing in the gap behind the eye, the man holding the short stick, inclined forward. There was a crack and, so it seemed, a roar of flame from the stick. One of the bowmen gave a wild cry, clutched his chest and pitched forward on his face.

The other *morlader* were running in wild panic. Cador would have followed their example had he not become aware of the girl running straight towards him, gasping and sobbing, tripping and stumbling because of her bound arms. The rope, still around her neck, was whipping and catching as she vainly tried to reach the shelter of the trees away from the vile, black creature which was even now settling itself in the clearing.

For a moment Cador watched the girl's struggle before he felt the adrenalin surge through his body. He sprang to his feet and broke into the clearing as the girl neared him. At first she thought a new danger threatened and skidded to a halt, almost falling to her knees. But Cador moved forward, unsheathing his knife, and crying: 'Quickly! I mean you no harm. I am a friend.' With a sob of relief the girl came onward.

One eye on the black creature, which now seemed to be disgorging men from the gap behind its eyes, Cador caught the girl and cut through the ropes that pinioned her arms, at the same time pulling her into the cover of the undergrowth. Once hidden by their shelter, he let the girl halt for breath.

'Who are you?' she gasped

He ignored the question. 'Let us get further away from - from that,' he said, jerking his head towards the clearing. She did not argue but turned and trotted rapidly into the dark shelter of the forest.

Cador hurried after her. 'What is it?' he demanded. 'What manner of creature can it be?'

'I do not know,' returned the girl over her shoulder. 'I have seen them once or twice from afar but what sort of creatures they are, I do not know. I only know that my father warned me to beware of them. They come from the east - they belong to the people of the See-ti.'

14

CHAPTER THREE

'Did you hear that, Yaghus?'

The young man paused, a frown on his handsome features. His grey eyes narrowed as he ran a hand through his long raven-black hair. His companion, to whom he had addressed his query, was somewhat older than himself. Indeed, the man had a craggy, almost ugly face, and his prematurely greying sandy hair was worn a little shorter than the young man's shoulder length locks. Frank Dryden, Yaghus - the healer, as he had become known during his year in Lan-Kern, shook his head slowly.

'I heard it, Pryderi, but I am not sure what to make of it.'

The two companions listened again but could hear nothing now.

'It must have been some animal, a *gourgath* perhaps?' said Pryderi. 'We are well into *gourgath* country here.'

'No,' replied Dryden. 'It did not sound like a *gourgath*.'

Dryden had encountered the fearsome creature before. In this strange world into which he had been precipitated from a fairly comfortable twentieth century existence, Dryden had come to the realisation that eastwards of Lan-Kern, that area of Britain which had once been known as Cornwall, the countryside was inhabited by strange mutant life forms - species of animals that had once been common to the countryside in his own time or that had once been secure in Safari Parks or zoos, but which now had mutated into strange and terrifying species. The *gourgath,* he realised, had been a lion but had evolved into twice the normal size with a sleek, glossy black hide and terrible staring eyes of yellow and two great sabre teeth which curved from its upper jaws over its lower. Dryden had been sentenced to be taken to *Esethva a Mernans* - the place of execution - to be sacrificed to the *gourgath* on the orders of Nelferch, the mad old witch queen of Lan-Howlek. He had only just escaped unharmed and the memory was still crystal clear in his mind.

'No,' he said again, firmly, 'that was no *gourgath*, Pryderi.'

Pryderi had spent all his life in Lan-Kern, the son of Kesmur, the high chieftain, and this was his first journey outside the security of its borders. For Lan-Kern was an oasis of normality in a strange new world. Within its borders there existed no mutant creatures or plant life such as grew in Lan-Howlek and which increased in dominance the further eastward one travelled.

'We'd best hurry on, Yaghus,' returned Pryderi. 'That noise came from the direction in which Kigva's tracks lead and, as far as I can tell, she is being closely followed by someone who treads more heavily than she ...'

Dryden bit his lip.

'Cador?'

Pryderi nodded.

Following the successful insurrection in Dynas Drok against the tyrannical rule of Nelferch-an-Gwargh, which had resulted in her death, Cunobel, the new *gwelhevyn*, the ruler of Lan-Howlek, had ordered all the sacred fires of the *drewyth* to be extinguished as they had been in Lan-Kern. They were never to be rekindled until *An Kevryn*, the sacred relic of the age beyond the time of the Great Destruction, was returned to its rightful resting place at Meneghy, the great *drewyth* sanctuary. Both Pryderi and Dryden had volunteered to set off after Cador and bring back *An Kevryn* to the now united peoples of Lan-Kern and Lan-Howlek.

For Dryden, however, the search for *An Kevryn* had begun before he had been captured by the men of Lan-Howlek and taken as a slave to Dynas Drok. He and Pryderi had ridden into Meneghy while the flames still roared and crackled after the destruction of Cador's raid. Mabon, the chief *drewyth*, lay dying on the bloodstained ground and, with his last breath, told them about the theft of the sacred relic which, to the *drewyth*, contained the meaning of life itself, the meaning of the very creation and man's place and purpose in the universe. He had raised a trembling finger to the fiery sky and whispered to Dryden: 'It is written... You will be the one - the seeker - find *An Kevryn*. It is your destiny.'

But for Dryden and Pryderi there was another reason, perhaps a greater reason, which propelled them eastward in their quest. *An Kevryn* might be a sacred symbol but Kigva, the beautiful daughter of Kesmur, was a reality. Both men loved Kigva and this love was the spur to their venture. Kigva was Pryderi's sister. And Dryden? Dryden had loved Kigva from the day he had first encountered her on that warm summer's day on the beach outside Kesmur's capital of Dynas Dor. He had loved her in spite of the fact that she had rejected him for the saturnine Teyrnon, the war-lord of Lan-Kern, who had been slain in Cador's raid on Meneghy. He still loved her with a deep, aching longing.

'Come, Yaghus,' Pryderi called urgently, breaking into a trot. 'That sound could not have come from too far away. Kigva might be in danger.'

Dryden was already following. He needed no picture of Kigva beset by danger to urge him into action.

Cador and the girl stumbled through the gloom shrouded forest and came, rather abruptly, to a large earthen embankment which seemed to be part of a large hill. It was covered with thickly growing gorse and dotted with burrows, large enough for a man to enter crawling on all fours. The girl stopped, gave a half-glance over her shoulder and pointed.

'Quickly, we'd best hide in here. Then the men of the See-ti will not be able to find us.'

Without waiting for Cador's assent, she dropped to her knees and, pushing a bush out of the way, crawled into the nearest burrow. Hesitantly, Cador followed. The smell of the animal came immediately to his nostrils as he entered. He blinked, allowing his eyes to adjust to the gloom, and then peered round cautiously. The burrow stretched only a matter of six feet before ending in an earth wall.

'This is an animal's lair,' he grunted.

The girl shrugged.

'I'd rather face animals than the men of the See-ti,' she answered simply.

Cador sniffed suspiciously. He had no way of knowing whether the burrow was still in use or whether it had been abandoned by its occupier - whatever that was. He crawled to the entrance. There was no sign of any pursuit so he laid his weapons by his side and squatted on the earthen floor opposite the girl. Even in the gloom of

17

the burrow he could see that she was attractive, with her long silver blonde hair. Her skin was smooth and creamy in colour, her features were fine and well proportioned. Her mouth was perhaps a little too firm, with a chin expressing determination. Her eyes were of a soft blue colour and yet conveyed an impression of fiery intensity.

'Who are you?' he asked after a moment's contemplation.

'My name is Onnen,' replied the girl.

Cador smiled. Ash-tree. It was appropriate in view of her willowy figure and long ash-blonde hair.

'Are you of Lan-Howlek? I don't remember seeing you in Dynas Drok.'

The girl pouted. 'Why should you? There are other places in Lan-Howlek apart from Dynas Drok. My father has - had - a farm in the northern territories, far enough away from Dynas Drok to live without fear.'

'How do you mean?' frowned Cador.

The girl laughed cynically.

'You must be a stranger to Lan-Howlek to ask such a question. You must know that the land is ruled by a mad old witch called Nelferch and kept in fear, and therefore obedience, by her grandson Cador. All Lan-Howlek fears and hates Cador who is the instrument of all our ills and discomfiture. There will be a day of celebration when Cador and Nelferch die. The people will come from all Lan-Howlek to dance on their graves.'

The girl said the words with such obvious hatred, and relish in that hatred, that Cador shivered. And the words shocked him. To rule one had to be strong and harsh. How else could a people grow great? Hardship was an obvious step in building a country from liberal decadence to a disciplined state whereby the people might survive and grow strong.

'Surely the people realise that sacrifices must be made in order to advance and become powerful.'

The girl, Onnen, laughed bitterly.

'Nelferch took a land of happiness and turned it into a land of evil and corruption.'

'But was she not making Lan-Howlek feared, making it great ...'

'Great?' Onnen's eyes flashed. 'People don't want greatness, they want happiness.'

Suddenly she frowned.

'But if you are of Lan-Howlek you would know these things unless -unless you were one of Nelferch's supporters?'

For a second Cador hesitated. He felt a compulsion to awe this arrogant girl by telling her who it was she dared address in such a forward and audacious fashion. No. He needed to ask her more questions yet. She could tell him about the *morlader*, the See-ti and perhaps even about Kigva.

'I have been away from Lan-Howlek a little while,' he smiled, disarmingly. 'I have only heard things by rumour.'

The girl tried to study his face in the gloom and then sighed.

'What is your name?'

'Cad ..' Cador bit his tongue.

The girl raised an eyebrow.

'Cad? That is an odd name.'

Cador gave a defensive shrug. 'That is my name. But tell me, how came you to be a prisoner of the *morlader*?'

The girl pursed her lips and grimaced.

'My father farmed to the north, on the coast. We awoke one morning to see the *morlader* ships in the bay. Before we could take up arms to defend ourselves, they were upon us. I saw my father killed. Others in our settlement were taken but I managed to escape on foot. For two days I fled into the forests but a dozen of the *morlader* came after me. Why they took the bother to pursue one girl I do not know.'

Cador knew; a girl with the beauty of Onnen was a prize indeed. Secretly he applauded the *morlader* sense of values. A few days ago, were he still war-lord of Lan-Howlek and Nelferch still ruler, he would have had this girl summoned to his chambers by Gwaun the slave mistress, just as he had done with Kigva. Kigva! He stirred uncomfortably at the memory.

'What then?' he asked. 'You see, I am searching for a - a friend of mine. A girl who inadvertently ventured far into the forest, journeying eastward.'

The girl shrugged. 'Well, I was captured just before nightfall yesterday. Beoc, the leader of the *morlader*, decided to make camp and one of their number, Conla, went off hunting. He did not return. During the night we heard a strange noise - it was the noise of the

See-ti bird, the creature of the air which you saw just now. It flew over us and apparently did not see our camp fires which Beoc had quickly doused. Then we heard the creature go down near by. There was a scream. I think the *morlader* thought it was Conla but, for what my opinion is worth, I believe the scream was too shrill ...perhaps a woman's scream. Then we heard the creature take off again. This morning Beoc gave orders to take me back to the coast where the *morlader* ships lay waiting...'

'I saw what happened then,' interrupted Cador.

The girl sighed.

'That is all I know.'

Cador plucked at his lower lip.

'So you think the creature attacked Kigva?'

'Kigva?'

'My - my friend.'

'Who can tell, Cad,' replied Onnen. 'I believe that it was a woman who screamed. If it was this Kigva, perhaps she was taken by the unearthly men who ride in the creature's body?'

Cador nodded thoughtfully. He had seen for himself that humans rode in the black grotesque flying creature.

'And you say that the creatures come from the See-ti?' he suddenly asked. 'What do you know of them?'

The girl raised one delicate shoulder and let it fall.

'What does anyone in Lan-Howlek know, Cad. Since my childhood I have been frightened by tales of the terrible *tebel vest* and other monsters. Among such monsters there have always been tales of the bogey-men of the See-ti who are used to scare children into obedience. But no one was ever really sure of their existence outside of vague rumours and a hundred and one embellishments of the imagination.'

'Well,' began Cador. He was interrupted by the girl suddenly reaching forward and laying a hand on his arm.

'Someone is coming.'

Cador's ears caught the faint swish of the undergrowth bending before the passage of a large body. His hand dropped to his weapons and he peered cautiously through the bush that obscured the entrance to the burrow in which they were hidden.

There came a low, rumbling growl.

Cador's eyes started in horror as he saw the creature, obviously the owner of the burrow, making its way with a lumbering gait straight towards them.

CHAPTER FOUR

Dryden and Pryderi pushed into the clearing and stopped abruptly. Sprawled on the ground before them were the bodies of half a dozen men - still and bloodstained. They had been tall men compared with the warriors of Lan-Kern or Lan-Howlek. All were bearded and dressed in garishly colourful costumes. Their weapons lay around them in useless profusion.

'What has happened here?' whispered Pryderi as he peered around with saucer eyes. A groan arrested his attention. 'There's one here still alive, Yaghus!'

The two men hurried to where a grey bearded giant lay sprawled. One look at the gaping red wound in the man's chest told Dryden that he was beyond help. He shook his head at Pryderi's questioning gaze. The young *drewyth* dropped to his knees.

'Who did this?' he whispered.

The giant's eyes flickered open and between grunts of pain he babbled in a language strange to them.

'Can you speak this language?' pressed Pryderi. 'Who did this?'

'They - they came!' gasped the giant, responding. 'My men - killed! Taken - they came in great bird!'

'Who did?' urged the young man.

'See-ti!'

The giant's head suddenly rolled back limply. Although his eyes still remained open they were already glazing. Dryden stood up and made a swift examination of the other bodies. Pryderi watched him with a frown.

'Yaghus,' he said slowly. 'Have you noticed something odd?'

'Odd?'

'In a battle it is not usual for the victorious side to waste time removing their arrows or spears from the bodies of the vanquished. The only weapons on this field are those of these slain warriors.'

22

Dryden said nothing. There had been a cold feeling growing within him as he examined the bodies of the men. He had knowledge enough to recognise gunshot wounds when he saw them.

'The See-ti, Yaghus!' said Pryderi softly, scarcely suppressing a shudder. 'If this is the work of the See-ti, then the legends may be right.'

He pointed dramatically to the chest of the grey bearded giant. 'Look at the burn marks around that wound! No spear or arrow did that. But legend says the men of the See-ti, if they be men, shoot lightning bolts at their enemies. Could it be true?'

Dryden shook his head. 'Not lightning bolts, Pryderi. A man-made weapon. A weapon that was used often in my world.'

'Before the age of the Great Destruction?' Pryderi was puzzled.

'There is nothing supernatural about this, Pryderi. These men were killed by a man-made weapon.'

'But how could such weapons survive the Great Destruction? According to our legends, that was many thousands of years ago.'

Dryden shrugged. 'We will have to find out. Tell me, what manner of men were these, Pryderi?'

'*Morlader*,' returned the young *drewyth*.

'*Morlader*?' Dryden scratched his temple. 'I have not heard the word before.'

'Buccaneers, pirates, who are said to come from an island north of here... Manawydan's island. For many years the *morlader* have come in large ships and raided our coastal settlements, although in recent years they have raided more along the northern coasts of Lan-Howlek, probably taking advantage of the anarchy that reigned there under Nelferch. They seize what they can - goods and even people.'

'But we are far from the coast here,' Dryden pointed out.

Pryderi hunched his shoulders.

'Three days journey at the least, Yaghus,' he affirmed.

'What could they have been doing here then?'

Pryderi made no reply.

'What now?' asked Dryden, after a pause.

'I have lost the tracks of Kigva and Cador altogether. I think we must work on the assumption that they have continued eastwards.'

'And these men of the See-ti?' asked Dryden. 'Might Kigva and

Cador have been taken captive by them?'

'Perhaps,' admitted Pryderi grudgingly. 'If so, our task will be difficult. How can we follow birds across the sky?'

'We are dealing with men, Pryderi,' said Dryden. 'They have somehow retained the use of guns, they seem to have the knowledge of flight still ... the things that fly are not birds. They are machines. And machines have to come down to earth sooner or later.'

Pryderi did not look entirely convinced. 'You say, Yaghus, that in your world - before the Great Destruction - your people had knowledge of flying?'

Dryden nodded. 'Somehow that knowledge has survived among these people you call the See-ti.'

'It is hard to believe. Nonetheless, Yaghus, we will go eastwards.'

Dryden smiled and clapped the young man on the shoulder. Without another word they cast a last look around the bloody clearing, turned and made their way into the forests once again.

As they disappeared on the far side of the clearing, a figure stirred. It was a black bearded giant of a man. In one hand he held a great double edged sword while tucked under his other arm - looking small against his bulk -was a black metal box.

Conla paused by the body of his former leader, Beoc. He looked down at the corpse without compassion and prodded him with his sword. There was no movement and Conla spat reflectively. He looked at the others and then cast an apprehensive glance at the sky. Sheathing his sword, he shouldered the heavy metal box and set off with great loping strides towards the north-west.

Clasping his javelin tightly in one hand and his long sword in the other, Cador scrambled from the burrow to meet the advancing animal.

'I'll try to hold it back while you get out of here,' he cried to the girl, Onnen, as she started fearfully after him.

Cador had led a self-indulgent and indolent childhood and youth. It was an upbringing that made him lazy in many respects; he would not do anything himself if others could do it for him. But Cador had one quality - he could perform every task that he demanded of his warriors. He was well trained in weaponry and could handle a sword or a war spear as well as anybody. Where indolence might have spoiled another's physical fitness, Cador was lucky in that his metabolism was such that his body never grew fat nor gross - although it was never sinewy. His eye and muscles never lost coordination. Above all, cowardice was an alien attitude to him. Cador was a man of contradictions; a man with many vices and several virtues.

Cador had never before seen the kind of creature that came lumbering towards him, though he knew it from the tales of warriors who had encountered such beasts before. He recognised it by its great size, its reddish fur and the way it now and then reared on its hind feet and waved two massive paws in the air before dropping back on all fours and continuing its shambling run towards him. He recognised it by the strange head which ended in a snout, almost like a dog's head, with its sharp, wicked-looking teeth. This was an *ors*. It could either rip a man apart with its muscular, clawed forearms or hug him until the breath was squeezed from his body.

As the creature drew nearer Cador could smell it, a vile smell which he could not identify. He could see its long shaggy hair and great hooked claws.

'Onnen! Are you out of the burrow?' he cried over his shoulder. He had sheathed his sword and was holding the javelin before him with both hands. At the sound of his voice the beast halted and rose up on its hind legs again, growling viciously and taking swipes at the air with its massive paws.

'Yes, Cad. I am behind you,' replied the girl.

'You'd best get away from here just in case the beast gets the better of me.'

'Don't be ridiculous!' snapped Onnen. 'I shan't leave you!'

There was no time to argue for the beast dropped to all fours, gave a bark of anger, and was running swiftly at Cador.

He thrust his javelin forward towards the chest of the creature but one great hairy paw struck at the javelin and snapped it from Cador's grasp. For a split second Cador felt a pain shoot through his arm. He had been holding the javelin so tightly that his arm had acted as the fulcrum against which the *ors* had snapped the wooden shaft.

Cador began to move automatically. He made a sudden sideways roll along the ground, away from the beast, and then scrambled to his knees, drawing his sword.

The animal had hesitated for, as the javelin snapped and Cador

25

had rolled under its menacing forepaws, Onnen had screamed in fear. The animal stood glaring balefully at her from tiny reddened eyes.

Cador came to his feet, his hand closing over a stone on the ground which he flung at the beast's head.

'To me, *ors*, to me!' he cried savagely.

The great shaggy beast lumbered around and looked at the puny man-thing that was daring to defy it.

It growled in anger.

Then it was making a shambling charge at Cador, stopping just short of him and rearing up to smite him with its muscular forepaws. Cador moved quickly out of range and the beast dropped back on its fours and came on again.

Cador's mind conceived the idea swiftly. It was obvious that, in charging, the beast had speed and strength. But apparently just before it reached its prey it had to rear on its hind legs to enable it to destroy its victim with its massive forepaws. The split second in which the animal rose from its forward charge to its striking position was a moment of weakness.

Now Cador waited, feet apart, sword ready, as the beast charged with a snarling, angry growl, towards him. This time he did not back away as the great brute began to rear up on its hind legs. Instead, Cador sprang forward, both hands gripping his sword hilt and, exerting all his strength, he heaved the weapon upwards into the creature's chest.

The great *ors* backed a pace, screaming terribly from its gasping, blood-flecked mouth. A huge forepaw swung. Cador tried to dodge backwards but something smashed against the side of his temple and his world suddenly exploded briefly into a multitude of colours before settling into a stark blackness.

CHAPTER FIVE

Dryden and Pryderi had left the forests far behind them. They had emerged onto a great plain which gave way, in the near distance, to undulating land rising to a range of small hills. Here and there a few copses rose in isolation but the plain consisted mainly of grassland. The grasses were yellow-green, hardly lush, and very short. In stark contrast, small clumps of mutated plants and flowers - in riots of bright reds and yellows - sprang up here and there, dazzling the eyes. Large flocks of sheep, wild sheep judging from their shaggy coats and from the way solitary rams watched over them, grazed peacefully. The sun was high in the sky and beat down with an intensity they were unaccustomed to, having spent several days in the chilly gloom of the forest.

Dryden examined the plain in mild surprise.

'I thought the forest stretched across the rest of the country without a break,' he said to Pryderi.

'There's a river ahead,' said the young man pointing. 'We can refresh ourselves there.'

They walked on across the grassy plain, which was spongy beneath their feet. They were less than halfway across when a rumbling sound made them pause and look round in alarm, weapons at the ready. Not far away the sheep that had been grazing peacefully a moment before were stampeding headlong, like some white gushing river, scattering across the plain.

'What is it?' cried Pryderi.

It was Dryden who spied the reason first.

'There! Look!'

Pryderi followed his outstretched hand. Just behind the stampeding sheep, a dark shape was bounding with a speed that astonished him. A strong, muscular shape which, even as he looked, overtook one of the stragglers and was upon it, tearing and shaking at it.

'A *gourgath*,' whispered Dryden.

Pryderi shuddered. 'I have never seen one before,' he confessed. Then, apprehensively, 'Are we not in danger?'

Dryden shook his head. 'The animal has killed its meat for today. It is unlikely to kill for pleasure - only for food. Let's go on to the river.'

They hastened onwards, Pryderi casting nervous glances over his shoulder every so often. The river was fairly broad but flowed sedately. Both men fell full length and drank thirstily.

'We can stop here for a rest,' said Dryden, rolling over on his back and breathing deeply.

'How are we to get across the river?' asked Pryderi.

'Swim.'

Dryden closed his eyes, feeling the warm rays of the sun on his face. He fell, almost immediately, into that curious half-waking doze, aware of his surroundings, aware of the fresh breeze and the warm intensity of the sun, and yet - somehow - in some sort of dream world in which he fancied that it was Kigva who lay by his side and not her brother.

The noise did not startle him for a moment. It was only when the implications of the noise registered in his mind that he opened his eyes and reached for his weapons. It was the rhythmic, coughing beat of a machine, a noise which Dryden had not heard for so very, very long.

'Yaghus!'

There was alarm in Pryderi's voice.

'I hear it.'

'It is the same noise that I heard in the forest, Yaghus.'

'Don't get up. Keep close to the ground,' snapped Dryden, his eyes feverishly searching the sky. He could see nothing. But the noise was loud now and Dryden knew what it was before the great black shape suddenly materialised out of the sky from where it had been hidden in the brilliant rays of the sun.

'Bel protect us!' gasped Pryderi, starting to his feet, his javelin at the ready. 'What manner of creature is this?'

'No creature, Pryderi!' yelled Dryden against the noise. 'It's a ... helicopter.' He had to supply the English word. Pryderi cast a blank glance at him. 'It's a machine, Pryderi. Not a creature.'

It was obvious that the men in the helicopter had seen them. The black, bulbous shape dropped rapidly towards them. Dryden could see the dark figure of a man balanced precariously in the hatchway pointing what was unmistakably a rifle in their direction.

'Put up your weapons, Pryderi,' said Dryden hollowly.

Pryderi looked at him in shocked astonishment.

'Without a fight, Yaghus?'

'You would be killed by them before they came within bow shot. These men carry weapons more deadly than anything you have ever seen.'

Pryderi hesitated.

'The lightning bolts?'

Dryden did not explain the difference but merely nodded. The helicopter came to rest some fifty yards away, sending a small gale whipping at their clothes and faces. A black clad figure was climbing from the hatch, another held a rifle unwaveringly upon them. Dryden dropped his war spear and shield and slowly raised his hands above his shoulders, palms outwards. After a moment's hesitation, Pryderi followed his example.

The black clad figure came cautiously forward. At the same time two more figures descended from the machine. Each carried some sort of rifle. They halted five yards away, the guns trained on the two men. Then, without a word, the first man moved forward and picked up the spears, unbuckled their swords and knives and took Dryden's bow and quiver of arrows. No man spoke.

Dryden examined the newcomers with interest. They were young clean-shaven men and they wore their hair closely cropped. He could not see their eyes for they all wore what Dryden took to be sun-glasses. They appeared to be wearing a uniform of black trousers and shirts of a gaberdine material and black, broad-peaked fatigue caps. They also wore black calf-length boots. Each had a belt on which was slung a holster for a side-arm.

Above each man's left breast pocket was a badge of some sort - a red cross on a white background. In his world the badge would have been the symbol of hospitals, doctors ... One glance at these grim beings dissuaded him from the notion that there was any resemblance.

The man who had collected their weapons now pulled some cord

29

from a waist pouch and motioned first Dryden and then Pryderi to lower their arms so that he might bind their wrists. This was done tightly and efficiently with their hands in front of them. While this operation was being carried out Dryden examined the guns the men were carrying. On close inspection they were unlike anything he had seen before. They had the same general shape as rifles but they seemed far more sophisticated and developed than the weaponry of his own century.

The first man was making a motion with his hand.

'*Cuman*!' It was the first word any of them had spoken. It was harsh and its meaning was unmistakable. With a half shrug, Dryden walked forward. Pryderi followed, wide-eyed but silent.

The three men closed in behind them and shepherded them towards the machine. Dryden had time to notice that it, too, was different from any helicopter of his own time. The first man was climbing in and waving Dryden to do the same. '*Cuman*!' he repeated.

Dryden, with some difficulty in view of his bound hands, climbed in and sat in a seat to which the first man had motioned him. As he sat down, the man reached forward and secured a seat belt. Pryderi entered, his amazement mirrored in his face. The first man treated him in similar fashion. Then the man actually allowed a smile to cross his sharp features and breathed something which sounded like '*gód*!' The other two men scrambled in and secured the hatch, taking their seats facing Dryden and Pryderi, their weapons slung across their knees.

The first man reached forward and picked up what Dryden recognised as an intercom and snapped: '*ráede*!'

With a startling abruptness, which caused Pryderi to wince and turn pale, the machine launched itself into the air.

CHAPTER SIX

Onnen gazed down at the pale face before her anxiously. It was now two hours since the man who called himself Cad had been knocked unconscious by the dying blow of the great *ors*. She had watched astounded at the unequal battle between man and beast and gasped aloud with sheer admiration as the man had cleverly outwitted the *ors*, leaping to its weakest spot and driving his sword through its great chest. But as the *ors* had stumbled backwards, one of his great forepaws had crashed against Cad's head sending him spinning headlong to the ground. A moment later the beast had expired.

Onnen had waited several moments before approaching the still, shaggy body and dragging the unconscious man away. She had made several attempts to revive him but the blow had been a mighty one and had broken the skin over the temples. She had found water, dressed the wound as best she could and then settled down to wait for nature to revive him. After an hour she had begun to worry; once, in her father's settlement, she recalled that a tree had fallen on a man and knocked him unconscious. The man had never regained consciousness but two whole weeks had passed before he died.

She looked at the dark, sallow face of the man. It certainly was not a handsome face. If anything, the man's features were swarthy and ill-nourished; his lips were too thin and she remembered that they appeared to have a habit of twisting into a sneer. But now they made his mouth look determined. She could not recall whether the man's eyes were blue or grey. His hair was black. No; he was certainly not handsome. But she found something attractive about his face - something that showed a depth of character. She would hate it if he never recovered consciousness like the tree-cutter at her father's settlement.

After a time hunger began to gnaw in her stomach. She looked at the carcass of the *ors* and creased her brow in a frown. There was food in plenty there and was she not the daughter of a settlement farmer? Within a few moments she had started a fire using flints which had been lying on the ground and she had taken Cad's sword, having withdrawn it from the chest of the dead beast, and determinedly cut a steak from its flank. Soon she was roasting the meat on a wooden skewer over the fire.

She had just finished eating when a low moan arose from the lips of the man. She knelt over him with concern and saw his eyelids flicker open. The lips moved and tried to form a word. She bent closer to catch it.

'Wa ... water...'

She had no vessel but carried the water from a nearby brook in her cupped hands. She made four such trips before the man was able to open his eyes fully and ease himself up a little.

He looked around him in bewilderment.

'What happened? Who - who are you? I seem to ...' He groaned and raised a hand to his temple.

'Try not to think now,' smiled Onnen, comfortingly. 'You had a hard blow from the *ors*.'

'The *ors*?'

The man followed the motion of the girl's arm towards the dead beast.

'I can't remember,' he said weakly.

'You killed the beast,' confirmed the girl. 'But in its dying moment it took a mighty blow at your head. You've been unconscious two hours and more.'

The man raised his hand again and tried to massage his brow.

'I killed it? I can't remember .... oh, oh Bel protect me!'

There was panic in his face.

'I can't remember who I am - or who you are!'

Onnen felt a surge of sympathy at the alarm and desperation in the man's face. She threw a comforting arm across his shoulder and wiped his forehead with a large dock-leaf. A cold perspiration stood out on his brow.

'Hush now,' she said, as if addressing a child. 'Your memory will return in time. You've received quite a blow.'

The man looked at her. 'But who am I? Who are you?'

'I am Onnen. You rescued me from the *morlader* a little while ago. Do you remember that?'

He shook his head weakly. 'No.'

'You told me that your name was Cad,' went on the girl.

'Cad?' The man shook his head. 'It means nothing to me.'

'You said that you were from Lan-Howlek. You mentioned being in Dynas Drok but said you have been away in recent times.'

'Those names are familiar. I am called Cad, you say?'

Onnen smiled. 'And I am called Onnen.'

The man shook his head again. 'I cannot remember.'

The girl sighed gently. 'Well, Cad, I suggest you sleep a while. Perhaps a good night's rest will bring back your memories. It is getting near dusk now. I'll build up the fire. You just lie back and rest.'

The man Cad lay back as he was instructed and for a while watched the girl as she hurried about the small clearing gathering wood for the fire. He still wore a perplexed expression when she came to examine him a short while later and found him sleeping a deep and natural sleep.

Onnen awoke just after dawn and found the man called Cad sitting up and poking at the smoking fire. She stretched herself and smiled.

'How do you feel this morning?' she asked as he turned towards her.

He shrugged.

'I still cannot remember,' he sighed. 'I have been up for an hour or so trying, but I cannot remember.'

Onnen inspected the wound on his temple. It was clean and already starting to heal.

'Well, try not to worry, Cad. Things will probably return to you gradually. In the meantime let us have some breakfast - then you must come with me to my father's settlement, or what is left of it.'

A tear suddenly stood in her eye as she remembered the *morlader* raid, the death of her father, the burning buildings and slaughtered animals.

'I cannot.'

She blinked and turned in surprise at Cad's low firm voice.

'But where else is there to go?' she demanded.

33

'I do not know,' confessed the man. 'But I know that I should be journeying eastward - I feel that I am seeking something.'

He frowned and scratched at his head. Onnen dimly recalled something Cad had told her before the *ors* attacked. 'Kigva...'

He glanced up at the name. 'What did you say?'

'You told me that you were following someone - a girl named Kigva.'

He ran a hand through his hair.

'Kigva? I should know that name.'

'It was the name you told me.'

'Yes, it seem familiar. I told you that I was following this girl? But why?'

Onnen's eyes narrowed. 'You did not say. Perhaps she is your wife?'

Cad shook his head. 'No. For some reason I am certain that she is not. But she does represent something valuable to me ... but what?'

The girl sighed deeply. 'Perhaps you should find this Kigva and she will tell you.'

Cad nodded eagerly. 'That is it. That is what I must do.'

Onnen turned away and made a face. It was none of her business. But the man had saved her. And - she felt some queer attraction to him, especially now that he seemed so helpless.

'You cannot go eastward alone,' she said.

'I must.' There was a desperate tinge to his voice. 'I only know it is very important and that I must do it.'

'No one has ever returned from the land of the See-ti.'

'Nevertheless, if that is where Kigva went, there I must follow.'

The girl stood up and went to the brook to drink. Her thoughts were whirling in her head. Surely things like this only happened in ancient sagas sung by the bards? Cad's urge to find the girl Kigva was surely unusual unless the girl was his wife? Yet he was sure that she was not. What then? And why should she, Onnen, have this overpowering urge to accompany this stranger into a land beset with so much danger? Gratitude for his timely rescue of her from the *morlader* and the men of the See-ti, from the *ors*? Surely not? Maternal feelings because he had lost his memory and was alone and helpless? Perhaps. But there was also something else - that indefinable chemical reaction which was called attraction.

34

And what else was left for her? To return to the ashes of her father's settlement now that he was dead, now that there was no one left there to care for her? Indeed, was anything at all left for her to return to there? Burnt earth, burnt buildings, dead people, memories. She was alone, totally alone. Maybe she needed this man as a crutch - maybe she needed the company of another human being, someone to give her a purpose in life. She finished drinking.

The man called Cad was grilling *ors* steaks over the fire.

'Very well, Cad,' she said, seating herself before the fire. 'After we have breakfasted we will go into the land of the See-ti and seek this Kigva of yours.'

CHAPTER SEVEN

Dryden looked down from the helicopter through the porthole by his side in amazement. For an hour the machine flew without anyone speaking, skimming over hills and plains where great herds of cattle and flocks of sheep grazed peacefully. It flew over great primaeval forests, before commencing to circle over another plain which was littered with the ruins of ancient, decaying buildings. All the while Pryderi remained silent but his face was white with tension.

Abruptly the helicopter began to descend, sinking rapidly towards the earth and then - Dryden caught his breath - a section of the earth seemed to slide back, revealing a dark cavern beneath. Into this, without faltering, the helicopter slipped. As it dropped below ground level the earth seemed to slide to above them. But there was no darkness. The cavern was lit by a blaze of arc lights.

The machine jarred to a stop.

The first man leant forward, released the safety belts, and poked them in turn with his gun.

'*Ut!*'

There was no need to translate the command. Dryden climbed out of the machine and stood looking about him in amazement. He was in some kind of huge underground hangar. Not far away stood a line of perhaps a dozen helicopters similar to the one from which he had just alighted. Groups of men and women, all clad in black uniforms, hurried here and there intent on various tasks. To Pryderi at his side it must have looked like some nightmare from the Otherworld.

'Yaghus,' he whispered, 'what is this place?'

One of their captors pushed him hard in the stomach with the tip of his gun. Pryderi coughed and gasped for breath.

'*Úp scyttan!*'

They stood there for a moment. The guards removed their black eye-pieces, revealing cold blue eyes, set deep in strangely pale faces.

36

They stared almost unseeingly at Dryden and Pryderi. Then a tall man, also in black but with silver bars on his collar obviously denoting rank, came forward and stood surveying them with a slight sneer on his thin lips.

'*Utlanders*!' he spat. '*Wilcuma tó* the *See-ti.*'

Dryden stared at the man in amazement. Had the man spoken in twentieth century English Dryden would have understood him no better than he did now. The few words his captor had spoken had certainly seemed familiar and understandable to someone with a knowledge of English. Did these people speak a derivative of English? Or was it some other Germanic language? How much of it would he be able to understand?

The man who had spoken turned on his heel, not noticing Dryden's astonishment. Perhaps it was as well, Dryden suddenly reflected as the guards began to prod him to follow. He would hold his peace until he learned the intent of these strange men of the See-ti.

At one side of the cavern, great metal doors slid back and they were shepherded into a large, brightly lit room. The walls were of smooth metal and, after they had entered, the doors slid silently shut. The leader of the captors moved to a metal grille. '*Tún seofen*!' he snapped. Dryden felt a slight downward movement. An elevator. He tried to give Pryderi a reassuring look. The young man was still very white but seemed to have his fear under control.

After a while Dryden felt the slight rising feeling which told him that the elevator had stopped. The doors slid open and they passed through into something which resembled a gigantic airlock. Dryden estimated that the elevator must have taken them a long way down into the ground - how far he had no way of knowing. Yet the air here was as cool and as fresh as on the surface and the light was just as bright without seeming to be artificial.

They were halted for some time in the airlock, their captors watching them impassively, until a voice came from a grille to their left, '*All riht*!' Then a second door slid open and they were motioned out.

Dryden's eyes widened in astonishment. He was looking at a busy city street. Brightly lit roadways radiated in all directions and buildings lined the roadways, most of them three or four storeys high. Above them seemed to be the sky - a blue canopy with white scudding clouds. Dryden stared at it very hard before he realised that he was looking at an artificial, vast projection of the sky. Only a slight flickering here and there betrayed it as a mere illusion. The light was strong and seemed to have no central point of origin. Groups of people walked or stood in the roadways, some looking towards them with curiosity, others taking no notice at all.

The airlock had opened onto a large ramp which ran downwards to the start of the street complex. It was vast. How vast, he could not tell. That it was a tremendous feat of engineering, a great city beneath the ground, he realised immediately. And then the thought struck him. City. See-ti. 'So that's it!' he exclaimed in astonishment.

'*Úp scyttan!*'

The blow from the guard caught him squarely in the back and sent him staggering into Pryderi who only just saved him from measuring his full length on the floor. The leader looked at them with obvious distaste.

'*Cuman!*' he said, jerking his head down the ramp.

Silently they followed him down the ramp to the streets. Dryden noticed that the people were clad in assorted costumes but basically modelled on the design of the black uniforms. The choice of colours seemed limited to black, grey, white and yellow. In the main, the people took no notice of Dryden and Pryderi as they were marched along the streets.

After a short time they entered a large building where countless portraits of a stern-faced man stared down from the walls. The photographs were surrounded by banners carrying the red cross on a white background. Suddenly Pryderi was hauled off down a side corridor and Dryden, under cover of the guns of his guards, was halted before a door. It slid silently open and he was pushed inside. Before he could turn around, the door slid shut and he was alone.

The silence was overpowering. The room in which he found himself was about six feet square and perhaps ten feet in height. The walls were an almost dazzling white and, if Dryden had not marked the place where he had entered, there would have been no way of telling where the door was. Everything merged so completely - floor, ceiling, walls. Dryden recalled the sensory deprivation techniques of his own time.

He stood still for a while, how long he could not judge, and then he backed slowly to a corner of the room and sat down, cross-legged, back straight, and closed his eyes. It was a trick which Pryderi had taught him from his store of *drewyth* learning - the art of meditation, of easing the senses, of calming the nerves. Nothing could be done until his captors decided to do it so it was futile to expend any more energy. Dryden shut out the glare of the white walls and began to concentrate on his breathing - slow, regular breathing, focusing on it all his thoughts and physical energy.

Cad placed a finger to his lips and shook his head at Onnen.

Then he slid down below the brow of the hill. Onnen followed his example.

'Horses,' he grinned.

The girl nodded. She, too, had seen the half dozen or so horses grazing upon the far side of the hill.

'What of it?' she asked, mystified.

'We'll make better time if we are mounted,' Cad pointed out.

'Oh? And do you have the skill to catch two horses?' the girl asked with a frown.

Cad's grin faded and he looked seriously at Onnen.

'My - my instincts tell me that I do, though I cannot remember where I learned such skills.'

The girl leaned forward and placed a slim hand on his arm.

'I did not mean ....' she began contritely. Then: 'Wild horses - it takes someone with great skill to catch and tame them.'

The grin came back to Cad's face.

'Perhaps I have that skill.' He picked up his shield and extracted from it a length of rope which he carried twisted by the hand straps. 'Sit here, Onnen, and do not move. I'll soon be back with our horses.'

She looked after him, her eyes filled with doubt. It was some hours before he came back, red faced and exhausted, but leading two fine mares still snorting and whinnying their protests and kicking at the ropes which held them.

'We'll camp here for tonight,' smiled Cad. 'Tomorrow morning I'll break these beasts. It'll mean a day's delay but once we are mounted we'll soon make up the lost time.'

Onnen had watched his skills at horse catching with amazement.

She had never seen a man as cunning and as strong. She smiled and set about building up a fire for the night.

Dryden heard the soft swish of the door sliding open. In a split second his eyes were open and he was on his feet facing the guard who was looking at him without interest from the doorway.

'*Cuman!*'

Dryden followed him out into the corridor. There was no one else about and the guard was walking unconcernedly in front of him. It would be easy to ... The guard halted before a door and pressed a button, speaking into a small grille in the wall. Dryden could not catch what was said but, after a moment's pause, the door slid open. The guard pointed inside and said something which was obviously an order to enter. Dryden did so, feeling, rather than seeing, the door sliding shut behind him.

The room was large and circular, its walls filled with computer banks and consoles. In the centre was a huge desk. Behind it was a man in the now familiar black uniform, watching him through half lowered lids. Exactly behind the man was a large portrait of the stern-faced individual, flanked by the red cross banners.

Dryden took a pace towards the desk. The man behind it was sitting stiffly upright. He held his head a little to one side. It was a calm, unemotional face, broad and with high cheekbones, and bronze hair brushed back from the wide forehead and cut very short. The eyes were almost colourless, though Dryden guessed them to be blue, and the lips were thick and red. It was the face of a man of about Dryden's own age.

He raised a hand and beckoned Dryden nearer.

'Come here, outlander,' he suddenly said, speaking in thickly accented *Kernewek,* the language of Lan-Kern. 'Come here and let us have a little talk.'

CHAPTER EIGHT

'Well, outlander?' smiled the man. 'You do not seem surprised that I can speak your gibberish tongue?'

Dryden merely shrugged.

'Well, no matter,' went on the man. 'I have interrogated enough of you barbarians to know that dumb insolence only disguises a mind of arrogant stupidity.'

He leaned back in his chair and gazed thoughtfully at Dryden with his pale eyes.

'Do you know where you are, outlander?'

'I know that I am in the land of the See-ti,' said Dryden, 'because one of your men said so.'

A frown crossed the man's forehead. 'How so? Only a few know this language.'

Dryden did not reply. It would not hurt to leave a few mysteries for this cold, haughty man to unravel. The man did not press the question.

'Were you told who I am?'

Dryden shook his head.

'I and the *thegn* Thaec. So, having introduced myself, outlander, you may tell me who you are.'

'I am called Yaghus,' replied Dryden, mentally noting that the word *thegn* was used as a badge of rank, perhaps it was the same as 'thane'?

'Yaghus?' Thaec's eyes narrowed slightly. 'That implies that you are a healer.'

'I have practised that art.'

'Where are you from?'

'I was a healer in Lan-Kern.'

'In a township or settlement?'

'In Dynas Dor.'

Thaec nodded and began looking at some papers before him. One of them was a map showing Lan-Kern and Lan-Howlek.

'Tell me, Yaghus of Lan-Kern, does Kesmur still rule there?'

'Yes,' Dryden made the affirmation automatically and then regretted it. He looked at Thaec with suspicion. The man caught the look and smiled.

'*Swa?*' The syllable was expressed in a sigh. 'You have some intelligence, outlander, but it will avail you nothing to play games with me. I know all about your country and about Lan-Howlek. We have long been investigating that area through our many captives.'

Dryden forced a smile.

'In that case there will be no need to interrogate me further.'

The man raised his head a little and laughed, it was a laugh without humour; the thin lips drawing back and displaying startling white teeth.

'I underestimated you, outlander. But you are right. We can extract the information that we want from other sources. You are just one of many captives brought to the See-ti to serve the people of the Cynn. Information is a secondary factor to your capture.'

Dryden registered the new word 'Cynn' and replied: 'And what is the reason for my capture? What service do you talk about?'

'You are here to work, outlander. That is all.'

The *thegn* Thaec pushed a button on his desk and, with a soft swish of sliding doors, the guard reappeared.

'*Tacan him tó tún án,*' snapped Thaec.

The guard prodded Dryden from the room. Thaec, bending over his papers, had already forgotten him. Dryden was propelled by the guard through seemingly endless corridors. There was no doubt that these people were speaking an offshoot of English. Or was it an offshoot? He had never been interested in etymology but, for the first time, he found himself wishing that he had learned about English word roots in order to be able to understand more of the language of the See-ti. Nevertheless, he knew enough to realise that Thaec had ordered the guard to take him to *tún án* - town one? Yes, that seemed likely. When he had been taken into the lift the guard had said '*tún seofen*' into the grille - town seven? Dryden smiled to himself. He knew this place lay deep underground and perhaps each '*tún*' represented a level? The guard marched Dryden through

42

the streets to the elevator ramp. Two other black uniformed guards took over here and the first guard turned away.

'Hey,' Dryden protested, 'What about my companion?'

The first guard ignored him but one of the others dug him sharply in the stomach with his gun and grunted the inevitable '*Úp scyttan!*' Dryden did not have to work out a translation to know what it meant. Coughing a little from the blow, he was pushed into the elevator. It was not long before the doors slid open and Dryden was ushered down a ramp into *tún án*.

It was the smell that immediately struck him; a sickly, sweet smell of sweat and body excrement. The guards had quickly donned masks. The rampway was ringed with numerous guards also wearing masks. The immediate general layout was similar to that of *tún seofen*. The broad rampway led down to a vast open level. But there the resemblance ended. Instead of the bright, almost natural lighting and the synthetic blue sky of *tún seofen*, here the lights were dim and flickering so that Dryden could barely see into the gloom. The sky itself was a metallic grey, smoothed and curved over what must have been the roof of an enormous cave.

As his eyes adjusted to the gloom, he began to get a better idea of the size of the cave which held the See-ti because none of the buildings on this level rose above one or two storeys. The great domed cave seemed to stretch into eternity. Tall metal towers rose at regular points throughout the entire complex and on the towers nearest him Dryden could see guards with guns. With a sick feeling, he realised that he was looking at a prison camp.

'*Cuman!*'

A guard pushed him towards a small building. A door slid back and Dryden was propelled into a brightly lit interior. Guards rose as he entered. One of them motioned him to remove his clothing and pointed to a shower. Reluctantly Dryden obeyed and stood under the shower. Cold, terribly cold, water hit his body causing him to gasp in shock. For an age the water played over his naked skin. Then, mercifully, the shower was turned off and he was led, breathless, into another room. Another guard came forward and made a cursory examination of his body. He stood back and nodded.

Dryden was led before some sort of camera, its shutter was worked and, after a moment, another guard came forward bearing a plastic strip on which, to Dryden's surprise, was his portrait, imprinted with a number. This was wound around his left wrist and sealed. Then he was handed a pair of torn, ragged trousers and a shirt and he was motioned to put them on. The operation had taken only a few minutes and Dryden's heart was still beating fast as he was led through another door into a small office. Here a little man, also in uniform but with some badge of rank on his collar, sat on a desk, idly swinging a booted leg.

'*Swá?* You Yaghus of Lan-Kern?' he asked in a soft, lisping voice. His knowledge of the *Kernewek* was bad. 'No longer Yaghus but Number Seven-Eight-Four-Seven-Eight-Nine. Understand? You here to work. Go to Block Seventy-Eight, Hut Six and report to hut commander.'

Another door slid open and Dryden found himself out of the building and at the entrance of the prison complex. Two metal towers marked the entrance but, to Dryden's surprise, there was no fencing around the complex, nothing to prevent the free movement of prisoners throughout the entire cave. However, as he neared the towers he became aware of a faint buzzing sound and felt a strange movement of air. One of his guards spoke into an intercom at the base of one of the towers. 'Block Seventy-Eight. Hut Six.' The current of air immediately in front of him ceased and the humming noise died away.

A guard pointed: 'Block Seventy-Eight is eight blocks along that path. Follow the path carefully unless you wish to be killed. When you enter Block Seventy-Eight the power will be switched on again.'

Dryden nodded. A force field? No need of fences.

The guard smiled. 'Remember, outlander, you are here to work. *Weorc macien fréo* ... work makes freedom.'

He pushed Dryden forward. Dryden could hear a humming and feel the air moving on his right-hand side. He followed a well defined pathway past signs which read 'Bloc 8', 'Bloc 18' and so on with the numbers being increased by ten each time until he finally came to 'Bloc 78'.

As he continued along the pathway he was aware of faces staring at him from the windows of the huts, sad, gaunt faces, faces that seemed no more than skeletons. There was something more ominous,

more cruel, here than anything Dryden had seen in the slave pens of
Nelferch-an-Gwargh. Here was something which impregnated the
very atmosphere with despair. He shuddered, wondering how the
society of the See-ti had arisen and for what purpose?

Each block had six long huts in it, although each 'hut' was built of
stone. He had no difficulty in finding Hut Six. In the gloom more
than a dozen men lay sprawled on their bunks. Dryden coughed to
draw attention to himself but no one moved or even cast a look in
his direction.

'Where is the hut commander?' he called.

No one answered.

Dryden looked round.

'I have been told to report to the hut commander,' he tried again.

Abruptly one of the recumbent figures let out a bitter laugh.

'Then you have a long way to go to find him.'

Dryden frowned. 'I don't understand.'

'You'll find him in *Hel*, outlander. He was killed this morning.'

Dryden bit his lip and sat down on the nearest unoccupied bunk.
A figure stirred in the shadows and came forward into the faint light
which filtered through a window.

'I suppose I am in charge now.'

Dryden looked up at an elderly man with close-cropped white
hair and startling blue eyes. The man's skin was taut over his frame
and sinewy muscles showed through his torn shirt.

'I am called Yaghus.' said Dryden. 'They caught my friend and
me today.'

The old man sighed and sat down on the bunk beside Dryden.

'You are of Lan-Kern?'

Dryden nodded.

'We are mostly Cynn in this hut.'

'Cynn?' queried Dryden

'Men of the See-ti. But I have been in Level One for some years
and so I speak your language, for there have been many from your
country incarcerated here.'

Dryden raised an eyebrow. 'So the captives of the See-ti are not
confined to outlanders?'

The old man forced a smile.

'No, my friend. Any who dare speak out aginst the Faeder or the

45

Witenagemot face life as a slave.'

'The whom?' queried Dryden.

'You have no knowledge of the Cynn or life here?' asked the other in reply.

Dryden shook his head.

'The Faeder is our ruler. The Witenagemot are his council of advisers.'

'I see,' said Dryden, a thousand questions in his mind. 'I would like to learn as much as I can about this place.'

'Save your energies for work,' cried a tired voice from one of the nearby bunks. 'Haven't they told you that only work makes freedom - and that is all you'll get here, outlander - work and more work.'

The door suddenly crashed open and two guards entered, dragging an unconscious figure between them. They deposited the body on the floor. One of the guards snapped out something to the old man, laughed and kicked at the figure and then both of them left.

Dryden sprang to his feet. In spite of the gloom, and the blood which caked his face and matted his hair, there was no mistaking the figure of Pryderi.

The man called Cad smiled gently at the ash-blonde girl who rode by his side. He felt extraordinarily happy and at peace. Once he asked: 'Are you sure that you did not know me before... before?' He gestured to his head. 'I still cannot remember but it seems that I have known you all my life.'

Onnen returned his smile.

'That is an emotional feeling, Cad. It is not a feeling based on reality.'

'Why is it, then, that I feel I know you?' persisted Cad.

'Perhaps,' the girl blushed a little, 'perhaps it is because our characters seem to go comfortably together. That is why we do not feel like strangers.'

Cad chewed his lip a moment. 'I wish I knew who I was,' he sighed.

'Better to know who you *are*,' replied the girl.

They were passing a small copse when a deep throated growl interrupted their conversation. A blur of yellow-red erupted from the undergrowth and sped towards their whinnying, fear-crazed horses. Cad strove to bring his mount under control, at the same time reaching for his spear. Out of the corner of his eye he saw Onnen's horse rear up and the girl lose her hold and tumble backward.

The horse, free of its rider, broke into a gallop.

The golden-red blur paused.

To Cad's horror he saw that it was a *gourgath*. Not a full grown animal but a young and vicious beast. It paused for a moment, confused between the fallen girl and the fleeing horse. Then it turned in the direction of the girl. The haunches of the young *gourgath* rippled with muscles as the creature gathered up its hind quarters for the short charge. Then, with a snarl designed to terrify its prey into paralysis, the beast began a loping charge towards the girl.

Onnen looked up, her eyes wide with terror and a hand to her mouth. She stood like a statue, unable to move.

Cad raised his spear, a sudden cold determination in his mind. He kicked his horse into motion. A few strides and he had cut off the headlong charge of the beast towards Onnen, placing himself between the girl and the *gourgath*. His arm went back and the spear flew swiftly towards the creature. The spear pierced the beast's right shoulder, causing it to bellow in rage but not to pause nor turn aside. Cad's horse, wild with fear, twisted away from the creature. Cad lost his balance and fell heavily.

The beast now changed its path and whirled towards Cad's prostrate form. But Cad was only momentarily winded. He dragged himself to his knees, his longsword in his hand. The beast came onward and, with a terrifying shriek impaled itself on the outstretched sword. The metal bit deeply into the creature's chest and its death was immediate.

Cad fell back limply, the weight of the creature on his body.

After a while he became aware of the girl sobbing and trying to push the heavy carcass from him. He managed to roll himself clear and found Onnen weeping in his arms. He comforted her gently and, after a time, her sobs died.

'Come, Onnen,' he said. 'We have to recapture our horses. They'll be miles away and it will be a long walk.'

CHAPTER NINE

'Pryderi! Are you hurt?'

It was a silly question. Dryden knew it as he knelt over the bloody body of his companion. Pryderi's black eyes flickered open and he tried to force a smile.

'Hurt?' He grimaced more in pain than in amusement.

'Don't talk, Pryderi.' Dryden turned to the old man. 'Can you help me place him on one of the bunks?'

Together they lifted the young *drewyth* onto a bunk. The old man brought water and rags and Dryden began to bathe the young man's face.

'He's been very badly beaten,' Dryden muttered.

'It is usual,' returned the old man. 'But he is young. He will recover. The guards are experts in beating people just enough to make them talk but not enough to impair their efficiency for work.'

Pryderi groaned. 'Talk? I - I did not talk.' The young man shook his head and tried to sit up. 'They asked me - asked me many questions, Yaghus. I refused to answer.'

Dryden laid a reassuring hand on his shoulder. Why had the *thegn* Thaec had Pryderi beaten and not him, or had Pryderi been questioned by someone else - someone not as subtle or sophisticated as Thaec? Dryden could do nothing more than clean Pryderi's wounds and give him water to drink.

'He will be all right after a rest,' declared the old man sympathetically. 'I have been here for enough years to see many survive such beatings.'

Pryderi had settled back into a sleep of exhaustion and Dryden and the old man sat on a nearby bunk.

'You have been here a long time?'

The old man nodded. 'Sometimes I think I cannot last much longer and yet I seem to survive. But the guards will spot me yet.'

'Spot you?'

'I am past the age,' sighed the old man.

Dryden shook his head. 'I don't understand.'

'Among the Cynn, my friend, all the aged, imbeciles, those useless to society, are put to death. I have survived execution only by luck.'

'What is your name, old man?'

'I am called Stigand.'

'There is much I would like to know, Stigand, about this world of yours.'

Stigand smiled bitterly.

'For you, Yaghus of Lan-Kern, there will be plenty of time to learn. You have until you reach the age of death. What is it that you wish to know?'

'Firstly, how did the See-ti originate? When was it built?'

'It is said that the See-ti goes back to the time of the Great Destruction. Yes,' he nodded observing Dryden's look of astonishment, 'we Cynn share the ancient legends of Lan-Kern in tracing our civilisation back to a time when the old civilisations were destroyed and man began to reshape the world.

'Our legends say that at the time of the Great Destruction, the most superior beings, men and women, came together to build the See-ti as a shelter from the destruction that stalked the world. Only those who were superior in mind and body to the rest of humankind - those who were obviously predestined to survive the apocalypse - were selected. The See-ti was built deep in the bowels of the earth where no harm could come to its dwellers. It was built on seven levels and, according to the social gradings of the people, all were assigned to their respective levels, starting with Level Seven as the ruling caste and so on upwards. But this, of course, is all legend. And the legend says that after the See-ti was built, the élite of humankind left the surface of the earth and came down into the See-ti to await the ending of the plagues and diseases that were ravaging the world.'

Dryden listened enthralled in spite of the circumstances.

'Anyway,' went on Stigand, 'let us leave legend. The See-ti, as far back as we have records, has been inhabited by the Cynn. That is the name we give our race. We are ruled by the Faeder, our leader, who is regarded as omnipotent in his decisions and his wisdom.'

'But,' interrupted Dryden, 'didn't you say that there was a council that advised your leader?' Stigand smiled.

'The Witenagemot? Yes. It is a council of seven *thegns*. Each level is ruled by a *thegn* and, regularly, all the *thegns* gather in council with the Faeder. But rather than advise him, in this age they merely carry out his wishes and see that his orders are obeyed on their respective levels.'

'I was interrogated by *thegn* Thaec,' murmured Dryden.

'Thaec?' Stigand grimaced. 'He rules Level Seven. A ruthless and efficient man who hopes to be the next Faeder.'

'But what of your present Faeder?'

'Aldgyth is our present Faeder and has been so for fifteen years.'

'Is it an hereditary position?'

'The strongest, most cunning, he who is able to eliminate all his rivals -that man becomes Faeder,' replied Stigand. 'And the Faeder usually comes from the *thegns* for they can exercise such power.'

'And has there always been a slave class in the See-ti?'

Stigand sighed deeply.

'No, my friend. All this -' he motioned around him, '- started three hundred years ago, according to our scholars. Alas, I was one of them. I was a student of history - once. Three hundred years ago Aesc was our Faeder. At that time Level One was given over to the growing of crops.'

'Growing of crops?' Dryden was amazed. 'You grew crops underground?'

'And still do. But not on this level. The See-ti had to be self-sufficient.'

Dryden wanted to ask about the processes involved but realised he should first learn of the social order of the Cynn. He motioned the old man to continue.

'Under Faeder Aesc things started to change. We had been in the See-ti for so long at that time that all forms of life outside the See-ti had been forgotten. Indeed, there had arisen a religious movement which maintained that there was no life outside the See-ti and its supporters even denied the existence of a surface. There was a great scholastic argument in those days. And then Aesc ordered an expedition to open the shafts which had been sealed for thousands of years. The expedition made its way up to the surface, not without some difficulty. When they returned they were blind. Generations of dwelling in artificial light had restricted their vision so they were unable to deal with natural light.

'Of course, the religious fanatics said it was a just punishment for defying their creed. But Aesc knew better. Protective masks were devised. Other expeditions went out. Gradually, over the years, we began to explore. Soon captives from the surface world were brought back to the See-ti. Their languages were learned and they were questioned. The old legends were proved. All this took time, of course.

'Near the surface, store houses - whose existence had been forgotten -were found. In them were discovered flying machines. But the knowledge of how to use these machines was also forgotten and the Cynn had to relearn it. What the Cynn have not been able to learn is the science and technology which went into building those machines. Only a mere half-dozen of the machines still work today and when these are no longer usable the Cynn will be unable to replace them.'

Dryden shook his head slowly.

'But surely the Cynn scientists could learn the secrets?'

Stigand laughed.

'Scientists? Ah, but I forget that you do not know our history. Well, over a thousand years ago - perhaps at the time of the first of the Faeders -there arose a great popular movement which maintained that science had betrayed the Cynn and that all the scientists were evil men who shunned the true religion. Led by the Faeders, this movement annihilated all scientists and only the technicians, those able to run the machines necessary to the life of the See-ti, were spared. For six hundred years science was forbidden, books were destroyed. Only in the time of Aesc, the most liberal of the Faeders, was science allowed to be studied again. But studied in what way? The old books were gone - destroyed. Science among the Cynn now is scarcely three hundred years old. There is hardly enough knowledge to maintain the ancient machinery.'

'I see,' said Dryden. 'But you were telling me how the Cynn adopted slavery?'

'The Cynn began to discover the world outside and, from captives, to form a knowledge of that world. Then, perhaps seventy-five years ago, Ulfketul became Faeder. It was Ulfketul who formulated the Creed of the Cynn. The Cynn were eventually to return to the surface of the world. This, said Ulfketul, had been ordained by the founders of the See-ti. While the lesser breeds had been left to the chaos left after the Great Destruction, the Cynn had been chosen to go into shelter and perfect their knowledge and wisdom, awaiting the day when they would return to take their place as masters of the world. Ulfketul said that the day was coming and that the Cynn would have to work for that day, training and perfecting their abilities.'

'An old dream,' nodded Dryden. 'Or nightmare.'

'At first the Cynn brought captives into the See-ti to gather information about the outside world. These were not released but given huts on Level One, where we are now, and utilised as crop tenders. Under Ulfketul it was decided that the Cynn should capture as many outlanders as possible so that all menial work would fall on them. This would then release the entire population of the See-ti to prepare itself for the task of world conquest.

'Level One has, over the years, become one great camp in which many thousands of outlanders are gathered. Each day they are taken to the other levels on which crops are now grown. They work until they die. There is no way of release.'

'And what of you, Stigand? How did you, one of the Cynn, come to be a slave here?'

Stigand pursed his lips.

'The Cynn regard all outlanders as racially inferior breeds. Breeds that have been polluted by the Great Destruction yet somehow managed to escape. Whereas the Cynn believe themselves to be pure, having been sheltered from the Great Destruction. As I told you, I was a student of history. It was my task to learn some of the outlander languages and try to compile accounts of their histories, customs and philosophies. The knowledge was to be used to enable the Cynn to conquer these peoples.

'In my studies I began to realise that the Cynn did not possess exclusive virtues nor the greatness of which they boasted. The Cynn were not superior beings. Indeed, cut off from the world and inbred through the centuries, they had -in many ways- become the reverse. I began to realise that the Cynn would be incapable of adjusting to the world outside, let alone imposing their views on others.

'I made the mistake of airing my views, of going so far as to say that we must release our captives and meet them as equals and learn from them. I found I was not alone in these sentiments. Some of my fellow scholars agreed with me. But within a few days we were arrested and asked to publicly recant our views. I was younger then and full of ideals. I had everything. I lived in comfort on Level Four. I had a beautiful wife named Edburga and a young daughter, Elgiva, who was only three years old at the time. Yet I would not recant. I was sent to Level One as a slave labourer and never saw nor heard of my wife and child again. That was ten years ago.'

There was a catch in his voice.

'And was all the opposition to the Faeder eliminated?' asked Dryden.

Stigand nodded.

'The Cynn have been preparing for a conquest of the world for seventy-five years, Yaghus. They have been perfecting the use of arms, of the ancient weaponry that survived from early times. Every Cynn man and woman from the age of ten years to that of sixty is equipped, armed and drilled. They are no longer a nation of individuals but one armed body ready to obey when the Faeder calls, or when the *thegns* or *eorls* decree.'

'I know of the *thegns* but who are the *eorls*?'

'They are immediately below a *thegn* in rank,' replied Stigand. 'Each *thegn* has twenty *eorls* under his command and each *eorl* governs a section of a *thegn's* domain.'

'Tell me,' asked Dryden. 'If the Cynn are trained and armed, what are they waiting for? Why have they not started this conquest?'

'Faeder Aldgyth has already issued the order. The day is coming shortly. The Cynn are ready. Everyone is now talking about *the daeg*, the day when the Cynn will start to march on Lan-Howlek and Lan-Kern. Aldgyth realises that the conquest of Lan-Kern would acquire for the Cynn great farmlands and grazing grounds and once these were consolidated and supplying the Cynn army, he could turn northwards.'

'So,' breathed Dryden, 'Lan-Kern is to be destroyed first?'

'Aldgyth has so ordained,' said Stigand with a bitter smile.

CHAPTER TEN

A strange wailing noise awoke Dryden.

The taut face of Stigand smiled down at him.

'There is no cause for alarm, Yaghus. It is only the call which gives us half-an-hour to report to our work parties.'

Dryden swung his legs from the bunk and caught sight of Pryderi sitting up and sipping some hot drink.

'Pryderi! How do you feel?'

The young *drewyth* gave a wry smile.

'I confess, Yaghus, there have been times when I have felt better. But I will survive, a little sore perhaps, but I will survive.'

Stigand handed Dryden a hot earthenware mug.

'Drink this, Yaghus. It is a *gyst* soup. I do not know what *gyst* would be in your language.'

Dryden sipped gingerly at the hot liquid. There was an overpowering taste of yeast. Of course, *Gyst* - yeast.

'We call it *gwel* in the *Kernewek*,' Pryderi said.

Dryden finished the soup and tried to ease the tension out of his neck muscles.

'I don't suppose you saw anything to indicate whether Kigva is a captive here?' he asked Pryderi.

The young man shook his head.

'Kigva?' Stigand interposed.

Dryden looked at him eagerly.

'Yes. We came eastwards from Lan-Kern searching for a young girl who strayed in this direction. A girl named Kigva. She is Pryderi's sister. Do you know anything about her?'

To Dryden's disappointment the old man shook his head.

'There is a separate compound here where the female slaves are kept,' he said. 'The Cynn segregates the sexes so that the inferior breeds do not bear children.'

'Surely that is illogical,' frowned Pryderi. 'If the slaves bore children it would be an easier way of replacing those who died in service

54

without resorting to capturing more?'

'Faeder Aldgyth issued an order that the aim of the Cynn is to eliminate all inferior breeds from the earth. Slaves may not breed and, at the moment, the Cynn find ample captives to replace those who die.'

'Can we get to the women's compound?' enquired Dryden, his mind still on Kigva.

'It would be death,' said Stigand, shaking his head vehemently. 'The force field separates the compounds. You must have seen it as you entered.'

Pryderi looked blank but Dryden nodded.

'Is it never switched off?'

'Only sections are in order to allow the slaves to go to the labour fields.'

'Then there is no way?'

Stigand scratched his head.

'Perhaps. We could try to pass a message to one of the women in the labour fields and obtain a reply in the same fashion during the next labour period.'

'It seems a lengthy method,' said Dryden.

'But it is the only possible way,' rejoined Stigand.

Another wailing noise, this time with a higher note, pierced the air.

'That is the signal for the work parties to form,' sighed Stigand. 'Follow me and do as I do.'

Eighteen men, including Dryden and Pryderi, formed up outside Hut Six with Stigand at their head. Across the vast complex of huts, others were lining up in similar fashion. For a short time they waited in silence and then a single note sounded. Each section marched off to predesignated points. They moved in an orderly, well-rehearsed, fashion with only one or two guards being forced to shout or cuff at transgressors against the rules.

Dryden and Pryderi followed the others of their section down the path through the force fields, which had been switched off, towards the elevator section. The elevator made a short journey downwards and when the doors were opened and they were marched onto the inevitable ramp, Dryden gasped in astonishment. The doors had apparently opened on a vista of large fields, clear blue skies and a brilliant golden heat. He looked vainly round for the sun but the heat seemed strangely diffused. The fields were tiers of troughs of earth containing curious growths. The troughs were placed in serried ranks - each a hundred feet long - rising up to four tiers three feet apart and stretching as far as the eye could see. Every hundred feet were constructions which reminded Dryden of liquor stills. Tired looking men were being marched from these 'fields' towards the waiting elevators.

'That is the second shift of workers,' whispered Stigand. 'We are the third shift. Each shift works a period of twelve hours and then has twelve hours rest. Each work period is named *timá án*, *timá twá* and so forth.'

A guard passed by with the usual '*Úp Scyttan!*' but the cuff was expertly dodged by Stigand.

Stigand's group was marched into a section designated by a number which corresponded to their block and hut numbers. They waited in silence by the troughs. Then a loudspeaker roared: '*Weorc macian fréo!*' It was a signal. The men moved slowly forward to the troughs, taking trowels and other implements, and bending to tend the fungus-like plants that grew within. Some climbed ladders to the upper tiers and continued their work there.

Stigand waved Dryden and Pryderi forward.

'We are on Level Three,' he explained. 'This is one of the food growing levels.'

'What is it?' asked Pryderi, nodding towards the plants.

It was Dryden who supplied an answer.

'Yeast. These fungi are some form of yeast mutation but they still resemble basic yeasts that I have seen before.'

Stigand nodded.

'You are correct, Yaghus. That is exactly what they are. I know enough of the outside world to realise that your dietary system differs from the Cynn. Because we have been cut off from the outside world for countless centuries, and have had to be self-sufficient in feeding ourselves, we have developed an efficient and nutritious form of food that does not rely on surface conditions for its growth. Yeasts presented our ancestors with a simple food which could be grown easily. Now all our food is yeast based and contains the nutrients we need.'

Dryden exhaled deeply.

'In my world microbiologists were trying to interest people in yeasts as an alternative food source, saying that one day we would destroy animal sources of food and the great crops such as wheat and barley.'

'I thought Lan-Kern had plenty of animals and wheat crops?' Stigand said sharply.

Dryden did not explain.

'How does this process work?'

Stigand pointed: 'The yeast culture is grown continuously. A fermenter has been designed with an overflow. Sterile medium is pumped in at a rate which is rather slower than the fastest microbes can grow. Once established, the culture continuously overflows into a collecting vessel.' He indicated the thing that resembled a liquor still. 'They can be harvested continuously. The microbes grow as fast as they are fed. The production process has the advantage that it can be automated, as it is now, and the harvesting can go on day and night and is less prone to contamination than previous procedures.'

Pryderi was looking at the Cynn in bewilderment.

'Does any of this make sense to you, Yaghus?' he asked in a quiet voice.

Dryden nodded. 'I'm afraid so, my friend. And,' he turned to Stigand, 'you say the whole basis of your food is now yeasts?'

Stigand made an affirmative gesture. 'It was the only way we could survive beneath the surface of the earth.'

A guard started to move along their section with a suspicious look on his pale face. Stigand thrust a trowel into Dryden's hand and turned to face the guard. 'I was just instructing the new workers in their duties,' he said, pausing when he realised he had spoken in the *Kernewek*. He repeated the sentence in the language of the Cynn. The guard turned, grunting the word '*Weorc*!'

'What about getting this message to the women's compound?' whispered Dryden as Stigand bent over the trough near him.

'We will have to wait for the meal break.'

There was no way of telling time and Dryden was beginning to feel faint with hunger when the siren sounded. The sections lined up and were marched away from the 'fields'. In a level and cleared area

57

were a series of benches. At least five hundred 'field hands' were converging in an orderly fashion on these benches. Placed at intervals along the benches were earthenware bowls and wooden spoons. Each section went to a pre-allocated bench and stood waiting. When all five hundred were standing silently, another siren sounded. The slaves bent down and picked up their bowls and spoons. They moved in lines to where women, clad in drab rags, stood by great urns, filling the bowls. The entire process was overseen by guards in strategic positions.

Dryden and Pryderi followed Stigand to where a large raw-boned red-haired woman stood filling the bowls. As Stigand gave up his bowl to be filled he bent his head closely and whispered rapidly in a language which neither Dryden nor Pryderi could understand. They caught the words 'Kigva' and 'Lan-Kern' several times. The woman looked at him through narrowed eyelids and finally nodded. Stigand moved on and Dryden waited while the woman filled his bowl with an extremely odious smelling mush, handing him an equally odious lump of bread.

The Hut Six section then marched quietly back to their bench, sat down and started to devour their meal. To Dryden and Pryderi, the food tasted foul but they forced themselves to fill their aching stomachs. When they had finished, the women brought casks of water along the benches for the men to drink. Every action was made in absolute silence under the watchful eyes of the guards. Then the siren sounded again and the men seemed to relax. A faint murmur of conversation filled the air.

Stigand leaned forward.

'We have a few moments rest break before going back to the culture fields.'

Dryden turned to him eagerly.

'What of Kigva?'

'I asked the red-haired woman, Gruoch. She has agreed to make enquiries in her compound tonight and let me know during the next work period.'

Dryden could not help feeling a little disappointed. He had half hoped that they would have been able to obtain news immediately.

'One thing, Yaghus,' Stigand continued, 'what do you hope to do if you find out that Kigva is here in the See-ti?'

It was Pryderi who replied for them both.

'Why, we will then devise some means of rescuing her and escaping from this place. We have to warn the people of Lan-Kern of the intentions of the Cynn.'

Stigand smiled broadly.

'Rescue? Escape? I am afraid, my outlander friends, that no one has ever escaped from the See-ti. Never.'

'Then we shall be the first,' replied Dryden with more bravado than conviction. Deep within him he knew that this weird city complex was like a great fortress - impregnable.

They worked for another exhausting period in the 'culture fields' before the siren made them assemble and march back to the elevators, passing the next work shift. Dryden tried to keep his eyes open, observing everything that could possibly be of value to any escape attempt. He noticed that to one side of the elevators were areas full of banks of machinery, with dials and controls at which men were working. In reply to Dryden's questions, Stigand whispered that these were the environmental controls and that each level had separate and self-contained control systems.

On Level One they were marched towards the entrance to the compounds between the two metal towers. At these portals Dryden saw a group of half-a-dozen black uniformed guards, one of whom was obviously a man of importance and rank, judging from the way the others seemed to fawn around him. Dryden noticed that Stigand's shoulders tensed.

'What is it?' he whispered.

'It is the commander of the slave camp, the *eorl* Gréne. I did not think that such an evil and sadistic brute could ever walk the earth. Since Gréne took charge of the slaves we have had no peace at all. He delights in our suffering, Yaghus. Have a care of that man. It is rumoured that he is an outlander himself and that is why he hates all outlanders. But that's a rumour. I cannot see the Faeder Aldgyth soiling the Cynn with an outlander's presence.'

The section marched slowly forward towards the gate, eyes lowered as they passed the group of smiling, black uniformed guards.

It was some strange feeling that caused Dryden to raise his eyes as he passed by - some strange, powerful pricking of his senses.

He raised his eyes and looked straight into the face of the *eorl*

Gréne and halted in mid-stride in total astonishment.

He found himself gazing into the equally astonished face of Lieutenant Green, formerly the engineering officer of Her Majesty's Submarine *Argo*.

CHAPTER ELEVEN

'We'll camp here tonight,' Cad announced, sliding off his horse and turning to catch the reins of his companion's horse while she dismounted. Onnen looked round and shivered slightly in the early evening chill.

'We must have covered many miles, Cad,' she whispered. 'We must surely have journeyed beyond the land of the See-ti by now?'

Cad shook his head as he unharnessed the horses and turned them loose to graze freely. It had been a week since he had captured and broken them and they were as docile as sheep.

'We've seen no trace of anyone or anything resembling a township, Onnen,' he replied. 'Surely we would have seen something other than this eternal emptiness and the wild animals.'

Onnen pulled at her lower lip and looked thoughtfully at him.

'Have you had any more thoughts as to who you are or why you are seeking this girl named Kigva?'

'No,' returned Cad shortly. Then he shrugged. 'Every time I try to recall some piece of my past life my head begins to burn like a fire. And yet ... and yet it seems I stand on the edge of remembering. Bel alone knows that I want to remember but some shadow ever stands in my way.'

Onnen sighed deeply and set about gathering wood for the fire.

'If only I could be sure,' she suddenly pouted, 'sure of what this girl means to you.'

Cad looked up, surprised by the girl's vehemence.

'Onnen,' he said, an expression of wonder growing in his face. 'Onnen, I swear you are a little jealous of my quest for Kigva.'

Onnen scowled.

'Jealous? How can I be jealous of something or someone of whom I stand in ignorance?'

Cad laughed.

'Onnen! Onnen!' he cried, taking the girl by the shoulders. 'I have known you eight days and yet it seems to me I have known you a lifetime. You have come to mean more to me - more to me than anybody else. I swear it! But I feel that I must find this Kigva for she can turn the key which will open the door on my past. That seems important to me, Onnen. But I will tell you this; I find that prospect not so important to me as this moment, as what you have come to mean to me. So if in three day's time we have discovered no trace of Kigva, then I shall return with you wherever it is you want to go. If you will accept me as plain Cad, a man without a background or a past, then I am well content.'

Onnen let herself be drawn into his arms and her moist eyes looked up at him, a smile quivering on her lips.

'Cad - I think I fell in love with you the first moment I saw you. I will wait three more days but if you are still no more than plain Cad at the end of that time, then I am well content too. It is for Cad that I wait, not his past but only his future.'

With that Cad folded the girl in his arms and kissed her passionately.

'Well, Doctor Dryden,' smiled Lieutenant Green, 'it's been a long, long time since I saw you last. I thought you were dead.'

Dryden faced the black uniformed former British naval officer in a small, brightly lit room in the administration block of the prison camp complex. They were alone. Green was relaxing in a comfortable chair on the far side of a desk examining Dryden with an amused expression. It seemed to Dryden that many days had passed since Green had seen him at the gate of the prison complex, had seen him and ignored him. Dryden had counted six work periods in the 'culture fields' and all his enquiries about Kigva had met with negative results. Then, without warning, he was hauled out of the work section and told that the *eorl* Gréne wanted to speak with him.

Green looked at Dryden's rags and shook his head sadly.

'Sorry I could not talk to you before, old boy, but I had to wait for a suitable opportunity without exciting interest.' His affected English accent rang hollowly in the surroundings.

'I gathered from poor Royston that you had escaped from the explosion on the *Argo*,' said Dryden, 'Also Harris.'

Green frowned. 'Is Royston still alive?'

'He was captured by the warriors of Lan-Howlek and died in their prison. I was captured later and was with him when he died.'

Green swore savagely.

'Warriors? Those animals?'

'Hardly animals, Green. Royston was the victim of a despotic regime which the people of Lan-Howlek finally overthrew. Anyway, what's happened to Sub-Lieutenant Harris?'

Dryden had a fond memory of the young officer whose cabin he had shared on the *Argo*. Green assumed a bland expression.

'Harris died.'

'Killed by the Cynn?'

'It doesn't matter,' replied Green. 'The whole crew of the *Argo* is dead except you and me, doctor. It's a rough world, a savage world. The weak die and the strong survive. You must have been strong to survive yourself, Dryden. I didn't think you had it in you.'

'And how did you survive, Green?' asked Dryden. 'How did you join the Cynn? I thought they disliked lesser breeds?'

'The Cynn? That's the Kindred in our language, Dryden,' smiled Green. 'Yes, I suppose that is quite a story.'

He tapped on the desk top for a moment as if gathering his thoughts.

'Royston must have told you how he, Harris and myself escaped from the submarine when she blew up? He told you how we were going through the forest and he went off to hunt and never came back? Harris and I thought he had been captured by the savages and decided to press on. We thought our best hope of survival lay in getting back to London. I don't think I really bought your theory about cryogenic suspended animation at that stage. It wasn't until we had traversed half of the country that I began to realise how the world had changed.

'Well, one day we were pounced upon by the Cynn. We were taken prisoner and Harris was killed. The first thing I noticed was their language. I expect it's been the same for you. I studied Anglo-Saxon when I was up at Cambridge and I found I could make myself pretty well understood. Within a short time I had a fluent grasp of their language. You see, the Cynn or Kindred must be the direct descendants of our people, still speaking a form of English.'

Dryden continued to stare at the animated face of the former officer under whose command he had chased Randall and his mutineers through the ruins of what had once been London.

'But how did you end up joining them - becoming an *eorl* in charge of such a disgusting task?'

Green gave a twisted smile.

'Very simple, Dryden. I was taken to see the *thegn* Thaec. He is a powerful man. He was amazed that I spoke his language. At first he didn't believe my story - I told him the truth about the *Argo*. But finally I convinced him. He said that if I came from the age before the Great Destruction I should be able to read some of their sacred texts. You'll never believe it, Dryden, but their sacred texts are some fascist books from the nineteen-thirties. Their society is modelled along the moral and economic lines recommended in these books!'

'I could see that for myself,' Dryden answered shortly.

'Well, Thaec was quite amazed when I read from the texts. *Aelmihtig!* Here was a man who could read the ancient texts to them. So they gave me a job. I showed them I was efficient and just as ruthless as they are. You have to be to survive in this world. Eventually I was accepted with honour in their society.'

'Prison warder to slaves,' sneered Dryden.

Green shrugged.

'What I can't understand,' went on Dryden, 'is how, with the racial philosophy of the Cynn, you became not only one of them but one of their hierarchy?'

Green laughed.

'Oh come now, doctor, racially we are of the same blood as the Cynn - they are our descendants, aren't they?'

'Yours, not mine.'

'Of course,' smiled Green sharply. 'I had almost forgotten that you're an American.'

'Do you know what these people stand for, Green?'

The quiet intensity of his voice caused Green to stop laughing. Dryden bent over the table, his face white.

'You said yourself, Green, that these people worship what in our day was called Fascism. Can't you see how evil and immoral that philosophy is? World conquest? Racial purity; slavery; the elimination of those considered to be of inferior breeds ...'

Green stood up now, red in the face. 'No, doctor. What we Cynn stand for - oh yes, for I am one of the Cynn now - what we stand for is powerful protection from aggression; law and order in a land of savages; power placed in the hands of those best fitted to use it; a people with the will and ability to survive in the face of adversity, in the midst of people not fit to govern their own affairs. Had we followed these philosophies in our own times, doctor, there would have been no age of Great Destruction. Our world, our society, was destroyed by its weaknesses, its toleration of liberalism. It will not happen in this world.'

Dryden looked pityingly at Green.

'I'm sorry for you, Green, or should I now call you the *eorl* Gréne? You're obviously at home here, truly one of the Cynn.'

Green glowered at Dryden.

'I hoped that you would join us. I have influence. I could have persuaded the Cynn to accept you. But you're obviously more at home with your savages.'

Dryden did not bother to reply.

'Very well, doctor. I will report your presence to the *thegn* Thaec. I am sure he will want to question you a little more closely than he has done before. In the meantime you will return to your hut and continue your work in the culture fields.'

Green touched a bell on the desk and a guard appeared at the door.

Pryderi looked relieved as Dryden entered the hut.

'What happened, Yaghus?'

Dryden raised a tired smile.

'He wanted to question me, that's all.'

Stigand came forward with a bowl of hot yeast mush.

'I saved your ration from the evening meal, Yaghus.'

Dryden did not have the energy to thank the man but thrust the mess down his throat as quickly as he could.

'I told you to have a care of the *eorl* Gréne,' said the old man. 'It is said that he has killed many men under interrogation. There is a rumour that in order to prove his worth to the *thegn* Thaec he killed his best friend - an outlander companion.'

Dryden felt hatred knot coldly in his stomach. Harris? Young Harris? Green had not said exactly how Harris had died.

'Anyway,' continued Stigand. 'It is only a rumour that Gréne is an outlander. And how can he be an outlander when he is a close friend of Thaec who, after the Faeder, is the most powerful man in the See-ti? No, Gréne must be a true Cynn.'

Dryden rolled onto his bunk.

'Let us hope your woman Gruoch brings us news about Kigva during the next work period!' he said abruptly. 'If we get no news, we must start making plans to escape from this place.'

Stigand gave Pryderi a wry look.

PART TWO

The Faeder Aldgyth

"Influence is neither good nor bad except in relation
to the one who experiences it. Some are moulded and
influenced by their loves and admirations, others by
their hates and hostilities. Is it not true that the shell
must break before the bird can fly? Is it not so that
our path through life is marked by the milestones of
our likes and dislikes at given moments? Living is but
the slow, wearisome process of being born."

An Lyver Mur'a Lan-Kern
The Great Book of Lan-Kern

CHAPTER ONE

The wailing siren urged the slaves of the See-ti to work. Dryden and Pryderi followed Stigand and their fellow workers of Block Seventy-Eight, Hut Six, to the great yeast culture fields of Level Three where the crops for the people of the See-ti were grown and cultivated before being sent down to other levels to be processed into edible foodstuffs.

It was the day following Dryden's interview with Green, his former companion from the twentieth century who now called himself the *eorl* Gréne. Dryden wondered how long it would be before Thaec sent for him to interrogate him further. He hoped it would not be before the first food break so that Stigand could have a further word with the woman Gruoch and discover whether Kigva was a prisoner in the women's compound. But whether Kigva was a prisoner or not, Dryden realised that he and Pryderi would have to attempt an escape soon, for the people of Lan-Kern would have to be warned of the terrible threat posed by the inhabitants of the See-ti. But escape how? The only method of travel between the seven levels of the See-ti and upward to the surface seemed to be the gigantic elevators.

As they travelled down to Level Three he asked Stigand about alternative ways of moving from level to level but the old man had never heard of any method other than the elevator system. One thing that had caught Dryden's eyes several times was the vast area of control panels and instruments situated near the elevators. Several uniformed technicians constantly manned this control area, watching dials and adjusting switches and levers. Stigand had told him they were the environmental controls, maintaining the life support systems of the See-ti and that each level had its own control systems.

'Each level is self-supporting, Yaghus,' explained the old man. 'The panels control the purification of the air, temperature and water supplies to the various levels.'

'Water supplies?'

'Yes. Each level has its own reservoir, great storage areas in which water is purified. The water comes through a filter system from the rivers on the surface but, of course, it goes through many processes to make it drinkable. All these are controlled at the panels.'

Dryden had a passing thought that if only the panels could be destroyed the Cynn would die in their underground city and the threat to Lan-Kern would be averted. Then he smiled ruefully. If each level was self-supporting then all seven panels would have to be destroyed. It was just wishful thinking.

The hours passed with incredible slowness as Dryden bent to his task of tending the yeast cultures. His mind began to spin with a thousand and one ideas and plans for escaping, each of which he discarded almost as soon as it entered his mind. At last the siren sounded and the slaves were lined up in their sections and marched to the rest-area. As before, the silent ritual was maintained, with five hundred men converging on the wooden benches, picking up their earthenware bowls and wooden spoons and waiting until the next siren sounded before shuffling forward to be served from earthenware urns by women slaves.

Dryden's heart skipped a beat as his eyes vainly sought the red-haired woman named Gruoch. But the woman emerged from behind a stand of urns and Stigand moved quickly forward. Dryden watched their quick whispered exchange and then followed Stigand back to the benches where, on another blast of the siren, the men sat down to eat.

'Well?'

Dryden and Pryderi looked eagerly towards the old man.

'The news is still negative, I'm afraid,' replied Stigand. 'For a week now Gruoch has made enquiries throughout her compound. There is no Lan-Kern girl called Kigva there. Nor have any female captives from Lan-Kern been brought into the compound during the last month.'

Pryderi exhaled slowly.

'So Kigva is not in the See-ti? She has not been captured by the Cynn?'

70

'It seems so,' nodded Dryden but Stigand interposed.

'That does not necessarily follow, Yaghus. This girl, Kigva, could have been taken directly to Level Seven. Was - was she attractive?'

Dryden's face whitened.

'What do you mean?'

Stigand laid a hand on his arm.

'Face the bad with the good, Yaghus. It has been rumoured that certain of the *thegns* and *eorls* take pretty captives directly to Level Seven for their own pleasures.'

Pryderi bent forward, his knuckles white as he gripped his earthenware bowl.

'If Kigva has come to harm -'

'We must get down to Level Seven and search for her,' Dryden interrupted Pryderi's threat.

Stigand gave a bitter laugh.

'It will be easier to escape from the See-ti altogether. Such a thing is an impossibility.'

'There must be some other way of moving from one level to another without using the main elevators. When the See-ti was built, its builders must have constructed emergency shafts containing stairs or secondary elevators.'

'I know nothing of such things,' shrugged Stigand.

'Are there no plans of the See-ti?' pressed Dryden.

'Plans?' Stigand thought for a moment and then nodded slowly. 'Each level has a plan which is placed by the atmosphere control.'

Dryden frowned.

'You mean in the control centres?'

'I'm afraid so. You will not be able to get near them. It would be a fruitless attempt, for you would be killed by the guards.'

'There's no alternative, Stigand. If that's where the plans are, I shall have to find some way of getting to them.'

'But they would only be the plans of this level,' Pryderi pointed out.

'Yes, but it would indicate if there were any other exits on this level. If so, there should be similar exits on the other levels.'

Stigand hunched his shoulders.

'Yes, but how are you to get to the control panels?'

'It's impossible,' said Pryderi.

71

Dryden smiled: 'Pryderi, you are a *drewyth*. Is there not a *drewyth* teaching that great tasks always seem impossible until they are accomplished and once accomplished are possible to all?'

'But - ' Pryderi raised an arm helplessly as the siren sounded for the second work period to begin.

Dryden followed Stigand back to their culture fields. The long corridors of troughs in which the cultures grew were traversed every so often by one of the black uniformed guards who made sure that no slave shirked his task. But the troughs were built in such a way that no more than half-a-dozen prisoners were in view at a time.

The idea came to Dryden suddenly, so suddenly that he did not even have time to consider the possible implications. As the guard walked past him he suddenly twisted round, his trowel in his hand, and brought it down with a smack on the back of the man's head. The guard crumpled to the floor without a sound.

Stigand stared at him in white-faced horror.

'*Aelmihtig!*' he exclaimed. 'What have you done, Yaghus?'

The other men of the Hut Six work force crowded round but Dryden motioned them to silence.

'I see a way of getting to the control area to see the plans - perhaps a way of escape,' he said softly.

'What is it, Yaghus?' asked Pryderi.

'Help me remove the Cynn's uniform,' replied Dryden, already busy at the task. 'You others, return to your tasks and keep a careful watch for the guards.'

Swiftly, Dryden and Pryderi stripped the uniform from the unconscious man and then Dryden took off his prisoner's rags and donned the uniform. It was tight but it was a passable fit.

Stigand looked on, perplexed.

'What will you do?'

Dryden gave a tight-lipped smile.

'I will walk up to the control area, look at the plans, and then return. Once I can discover an alternative way out of this level we can make our plans for an escape.'

'It is too simple,' replied Stigand.

'It is the simple things that work best,' remarked Pryderi, nodding his approval. 'Is there anything we can do, Yaghus?'

'Just keep a careful watch on the guard. Make sure he doesn't

72

return to consciousness until I get back.'

Dryden straightened up, hitched the gun into the crook of his arm and sauntered nonchalantly along the aisle between the troughs, thankfully meeting no other guards in that section. He came to the end of the troughs and saw the broad ramp which led to the elevators. Groups of guards stood about but no one took any notice of him.

He swallowed nervously and then, with a purposeful stride, he walked swiftly towards the ramp in the direction of the control panels which stretched away to the left of the elevator entrances. He was not challenged as he walked up the ramp past the elevators - which he noticed were well guarded - and along a broad concrete walkway which fronted onto the control area. A guard was lounging at the entrance of a railed-off section which was where the main control units appeared to be. Half-a-dozen men were watching dials and indicators. One of them turned to give Dryden an unfriendly stare.

'*Gód daeg*,' said Dryden, using the phrase he had heard the men of the Cynn greet one another with. It was close enough to 'good day' for Dryden to understand the meaning. The man grunted in reply and took no more notice as Dryden walked by.

As he moved forward Dryden's eyes swiftly searched the control columns before him. There was nothing there to indicate which were the atmosphere controls. He realised he should have asked Stigand for more exact instructions. Stigand had merely said that the plan was 'by the atmosphere control'. All Dryden could see was a series of brightly coloured indicators and dials all looking pretty much alike. Then he caught sight of a white rectangular board further down on a central panel. Yes - it was a plan of some sort. He moved forward eagerly.

'*Hwaet willa éow hér?*'

A harsh voice halted him in mid-stride. An attendant had turned from his dials and was regarding him with intense suspicion.

Dryden summoned a smile and muttered '*Gód daeg.*'

The greeting was not returned.

'*Hwaet willa éow hér?*' repeated the man. Dryden could work out that the man was asking 'What will you here?' or 'What are you doing here?' but he had no reply.

The man turned and abruptly cried: '*Weardian - cuman hér!*'

In desperation Dryden sprang forward, trying to reach the plan. At least, if he was to be recaptured, he must first get a glance at the layout of the level. But the attendant had gripped him by the arm. Dryden tried to prise himself loose and push forward. He could hear shouts now and the sound of running feet.

Too late he remembered the weapon he carried and tried to free his arms. A guard had arrived to help the attendant and Dryden felt a blow in the middle of his back which knocked all the breath and fight from his body. He fell to the floor, on his hands and knees, his head swimming. A boot caught him in the side causing him to gasp in agony.

'*Up standan!*' snarled a voice. The order was punctuated by another kick which landed on his thigh. Reluctantly he rose to his feet. The attendant was leaning forward and screaming at him. Dryden shook his head and mumbled that he did not understand.

'*Swá?*' breathed the man frowning. He stood back, hands on hips. Then he turned and snapped something to a third man, pointing to a badge on the collar of Dryden's uniform. The man nodded and ran off.

A thin faced guard, with badges of rank, came up and questioned the attendant. Dryden saw that the attendant now stood stiffly to attention and responded each time with '*min eorl*' before replying. From this Dryden realised, with a curious detachment, that the man was the officer in command of the guards of this section. The *eorl* finished his questions and then turned to examine Dryden. He drew his lips back in a curious smile, using no other facial muscles.

'You are a slave.' He spoke in the *Kernewek*.

It was a statement. Dryden did not bother to reply.

'Answer!' snapped the man.

Just then the guard who had been sent on some errand by the attendant returned, snapped to attention and spoke rapidly. The *eorl* grinned evilly at Dryden.

'*Swá?* You are Seven-Eight-Four-Seven-Eight-Nine of Block Seventy-eight, Hut Six?'

Dryden made no reply.

The thin faced man gave a half nod. There was a sudden blinding pain and Dryden found himself on his knees before the *eorl*. Hands dragged him back to his feet.

'You will respond, please,' smiled the *eorl*.

'Yes,' grunted Dryden.

'You knocked *Weardian* Eadsige unconscious and stole his uniform. You attempted to escape.'

Dryden nodded.

'You will please tell me who were the other conspirators in this futile attempt?'

'No one. I acted alone.'

The blow was struck again and this time Dryden measured his full length on the ground, blood streamed from cuts on his face and he felt sick. Again, he was hauled to his feet.

'Who else aided you?'

'I was alone.'

The *eorl* held up a hand, as if to stay an unseen blow.

'Very well - I believe you. Well, Seven-Eight-Four-Seven-Eight-Nine, what you have done merits death. You have also earned seven days solitary confinement with no food or water for all your colleagues in Hut Six. But for you there is mercy - a painless death now.'

Dryden found himself gripped by the arms and dragged swiftly away from the control area, across to the open patch before the culture fields. Just in front of the elevator ramp was an eight foot high concrete block. Embedded in the concrete were four metal rings. Two at the bottom and two at the top. He found his arms stretched upwards and tied by means of short ropes to the top metal rings while his ankles were similarly secured to those below.

The guards moved to a position ten yards away, facing him and unslinging their weapons.

Dryden felt a stunned disbelief as the thin faced *eorl* moved to a position by their side.

'Your body will be a lesson to the rest of the slave workers when their work period is up,' he sneered. Then he turned to the guards.

'*Weardian - ráede*?'

Dryden felt a surge of nausea and then blackness.

CHAPTER TWO

Dryden's first thought when he recovered consciousness was: 'Is this death?'

He was lying on a couch in a dimly lit room. The couch was soft and comfortable. The walls of the room were bare but soaked in soft golden lights which mingled and merged with each other in strange billowing movements which were both pleasing to the eye and soporific.

He raised himself on an elbow and groaned as a wave of dizziness surged through his head. He put up a hand to massage his brow and succeeded in clearing it. He realised that he had been washed and his cuts were dressed. He was clad in a white towelling robe.

The thought finally registered: he had not died. But what had happened? Where was he?

A door slid open with a faint hiss and a bald man entered. He was dressed in white and carried a tray. He said nothing but went to a wall near the couch and pressed a button. Out of the wall slid a small platform at the height of a man's waist. On this the man placed his tray. He turned and went back to the door, which obediently slid open once again. On the threshold he turned and pointed to the tray.

'*Etan*!' he ordered and was gone.

Still rubbing his head, Dryden looked dubiously at the tray. There was a carafe of water, obviously ice cold for condensation was forming on the glass. The plate of food was hot and Dryden could smell the tang of yeast. He forced himself to eat it; it was best to eat food when it was provided for one never knew where another meal might come from.

Some while later the bald man returned. This time he carried some clothes with him, nondescript overalls of white material. He motioned to Dryden to put them on.

'Where am I?' demanded Dryden in English.

The man started and frowned.

'*Tún seofen*,' he grunted, obviously having understood.

Level Seven! Kigva! The thought immediately crowded his mind. Then other thoughts clamoured for attention. Why had he been brought down here? His mind turned over the events on Level Three. He had finished dressing when, almost on cue, the bald man appeared for a third time. He waved Dryden forward and he found himself following the man into a large corridor along which people were hurrying in both directions. At regular intervals down the middle of this corridor were comfortable-looking benches on which some people reclined and conversed with each other.

Dryden and his guide left the main corridor and moved into a smaller passageway whose entrance was guarded by two black uniformed *weardian* or guardians. Along this corridor, every fifty yards or so stood other *weardian*, weapons loosely held across their chests, eyes alert. The bald man stopped at a door which, at some hidden signal, slid open.

The handsome, bronze-haired figure of the *thegn* Thaec came forward to greet them. He was smiling broadly.

'Ah, Dryden - so you have played a game with us? But enter.' He turned to the bald man and spoke rapidly, addressing the man as Wulfnoth. The man nodded and left, the door hissing shut behind him. Thaec, like an old friend, placed his hand under Dryden's arm and drew him into the room. It was large and furnished with some degree of comfort, a breathtaking mixture of modern luxury and barbaric rudeness. 'This is my apartment,' explained Thaec.

Dryden eyed the *thegn* narrowly.

'Why wasn't I killed?' he demanded.

'Did you want to die?' countered the *thegn* with a smile.

'Don't play games with me,' said Dryden.

Thaec shrugged.

'If the *eorl* of Culture Field Twelve had had his way you would have been dead some hours ago. But, thanks be to the *Aelmihtig*, my messenger arrived just in time to save you from the *eorl's* firing squad. You are a fool, Dryden.'

Dryden suddenly realised the implication of the *thegn* using his correct name.

'So you have spoken to Green?'

'Green? Ah yes, Gréne. Why didn't you tell me the truth when you came to the See-ti?'

Dryden shrugged; 'Why should I?'

Thaec raised an eyebrow: 'Yes, there was no reason. But it would have made things a little better for you.'

'How so?'

'You are obviously not one of the barbarian races that populate the surface. The language that Gréne and you speak has many similarities with the language of the Cynn. Gréne has spent some hours instructing me in its structure. It would seem our peoples were, at one time, the same. Why not take your place as part of our civilisation as Gréne has done?'

Dryden sat down, uninvited, on a chair. It was covered in some animal fur and was warm and comfortable.

'What if I do not like your so-called civilisation?'

Thaec laughed in amusement.

'That would be only because you do not know it.'

A thought suddenly entered Dryden's mind, causing him to feel guilty that it had not occurred before.

'Before we continue further - what of my colleagues in Block Seventy-Eight Hut Six?'

'What of them?'

'The *eorl* said he was going to shut them in solitary confinement without food or water for seven days. They had nothing to do with my escape attempt. And now, if I am not to be punished for it, neither should they be punished.'

The *thegn* turned to an instrument on his desk, flicked a switch and delivered what was obviously a string of orders. Then he smiled blandly at Dryden.

'Your colleagues, as you call them, will not be punished.'

Dryden felt relief.

'But now, favour for favour, Dryden ... I want you to tell me your story.'

There was no harm in that, thought Dryden, and it was clear that Thaec wanted to compare it with Green's account. Dryden sat back and briefly told him how the submarine *Argo* had sunk out of control under the Arctic seas in the twentieth century, how everyone had lost consciousness, and when they came to and managed to surface, their world was no more. Instead they had emerged into a strange, new world. Dryden added that they had come to the conclusion that they had gone through a form of cryogenic suspended animation for hundreds or thousands of years; time enough for their world to change. He went on, with only minor interruptions from Thaec seeking to clarify points, recounting how they had brought the submarine, which was badly damaged, down to the area which had been Cornwall. Finally, Dryden told how he had been alone on shore one day when the submarine had blown up leaving him - so he had thought at the time - alone in the new world.

'After that I lived for a year in Lan-Kern where, because of my botanical knowledge, I was able to use plants to cure ailments and so I became a healer. It was a society into which I decided to settle. Their way of life, their culture and philosophy, was pleasing to me.'

Thaec scowled.

'Culture? Philosophy? You claim that a sub-species possesses such attributes? Nonsense! Here, in the See-ti, is the only real culture left in the world. This is civilisation, the surface peoples are just half-breed animals, an infestation that will be wiped from ...'

He paused in his tirade and smiled. 'Ah, I see. There is an ancient saying among the Cynn. In the country of the blind the one-eyed man is king. Perhaps you, possessed of knowledge and civilisation, saw your way clear to becoming emperor of those savages?'

Dryden did not bother to reply.

Thaec sat smiling a while. '*Swá?* Your story, incredible as it seems, is precisely the same as that recounted by Gréne.'

'You had doubts about Green's story?' queried Dryden.

'Some,' admitted the *thegn*. 'What else could we experience but doubt when faced with such a tale?'

'And yet you allowed him to join your -' Dryden grimaced with distaste - 'master race?'

'Gréne proved to be a useful person.'

'A pity you did not realise that when you captured Green and killed young Harris.'

Thaec raised an eyebrow.

'Killed Harris? You mean the young man who was Gréne's companion?'

Dryden nodded.

'But it was Gréne himself who killed Harris,' Thaec smiled. 'We captured them both and, after interrogation, we felt we could learn much from them. We realised they were not of the barbarian species on the surface but we were not sure who they were. We offered them freedom within the See-ti. Harris, the young man, refused. Gréne was more cooperative. He bargained that if he proved himself strong and ruthless enough to be regarded as a Cynn then, in return, we would place him in a position of power. The proof he offered was the ability to turn, without compunction or remorse, and kill his companion. Indeed, he showed all the strength of a Cynn warrior - strength, the elimination of the petty emotions which hamper lesser breeds.'

Dryden gripped the edge of his chair and felt a cold fury sweep through him. So it was Green who had killed young Harris.

'And now, Dryden,' Thaec was saying, 'I would like to show you something of the See-ti because I am sure that you will join us when you realise just what the Cynn mean. There is much you can offer us and much with which we can reward you. Soon, very soon now, the armies of the Cynn will finally emerge on the surface of the world once again. For generations we have been perfecting shields to guard our eyes against the outside light and training many of our warriors to adapt to the light without shields. It was a long, wearisome process, but we are nearly ready. Now we can move forward and begin to implement our great design, to fulfil our destiny, to control the surface so that we can begin a new life, so that our people, those who have descended from the selected few who went down into the See-ti at the time of the Great Destruction, will inherit the world as it was ordained by the *Aelmihtig*!'

Dryden looked at the fanatical expression on Thaec's face and suppressed a shiver. With his mind working quickly he realised that it would be useful to allow Thaec to show him the See-ti and not to antagonise the man. Perhaps in this way he might be able to discover if Kigva was a prisoner somewhere on Level Seven and whether there was some way in which an escape might be effected from this weird world of the Cynn.

He followed Thaec's example and rose to his feet.

'I am ready,' he said.

Thaec nodded approval.

'I am pleased you are not given to making futile gestures as your countryman Harris was. I would have had to hand you over to Gréne in order that he might demonstrate his loyalty to us once more.'

'Where will this tour begin?' asked Dryden, ignoring the threat.

'Why not here in *Tún seofen*?' suggested Thaec.

'Would it not be best to describe the layout of the level before we start?' suggested Dryden, realising the possibility of finding an escape route. He tried to hold back the quiver of excitement in his voice, wondering whether Thaec would fall for his seemingly innocent request.

'That is a wise idea,' commented the *thegn*, moving to a cupboard and taking from it a folded sheet of paper. Dryden felt a surge of adrenalin as the *thegn* made to unfold it.

The door slid open and a guard stepped into the room, stiffening to attention.

'The Faeder' he cried.

Thaec snapped to attention. Dryden turned bemused as a man of medium height and lean carriage strode through the doorway followed by a retinue of half-a-dozen men in various kinds of uniform. The man pulled up short when he saw Dryden and scowled deeply. Dryden recognised the face from the countless portraits that bedecked the levels of the See-ti. He had come face to face with the absolute ruler of the Cynn.

CHAPTER THREE

Aldgyth, Faeder of the Cynn, and absolute ruler of the See-ti, stared disdainfully at Dryden. He was a fair-haired man with large, watery blue eyes. The face was fleshy and dark around the eyes, and there was a nervous tic in his cheek. He kept his hands clasped behind him as though to prevent them from twisting nervously. He snapped out a question at Thaec who moved forward and replied in a deferential tone.

Aldgyth turned his hypnotic, large eyes upon Dryden. Dryden returned the stare.

'The outlander is not of Lan-Kern, *mín Faeder*,' said Thaec, speaking in the *Kernewek*, presumably so that Dryden could understand. 'He is of the same strange race as the *eorl* Gréne.'

The Faeder's pudgy face screwed into a frown.

'*Swá*? Is this outlander gibberish the only other tongue you speak apart from your own, outlander?' asked Aldgyth.

'Yes,' responded Dryden.

'Where is this land you come from?'

'It is a land that is no more, an age that is no more,' replied Dryden indifferently.

Aldgyth's eyes switched to Thaec.

'Does the man support Gréne's story?'

'Yes, *mín Faeder*.'

'It is difficult to believe. And the man also speaks the same tongue as Gréne?'

'Yes, *mín Faeder*.'

'*Swá?*'

Aldgyth turned back to the door as if he had suddenly lost all interest in the matter. One of his aides whispered something to him and Aldgyth turned back to Thaec and spoke rapidly to him. The *thegn* nodded. The Faeder of the Cynn turned again and left with his entourage trailing behind him. Thaec stood for a moment looking at the closed door with a curious expression in his eyes.

Dryden interpreted the expression at once.

'You do not seem to like this Aldgyth?' he murmured.

Thaec turned, altering his facial expression like a small boy caught stealing jam. Dryden caught the flicker of fear in the man's eyes.

'What do you mean, outlander?'

'Your face betrays you, Thaec. Is it fear or is it jealousy?'

Thaec turned with a snort, picked up the plan of the See-ti and replaced it in the cupboard. As if at some signal the door opened and the bald-headed Wulfnoth entered.

'We will continue this conversation later, Dryden. I am summoned to the Witenagemot, the parliament of the See-ti.'

Pryderi cast a gloomy look around the interior of Hut Six and sighed.

'What do you think they have done with Yaghus?' he asked of no one in particular.

'Killed him. What else?' grunted one of the men from his bunk.

'It was a stupid thing to attempt,' responded a man named Rudhyk, who had once been a shepherd on the borderlands of Lan-Howlek and had spent the last four years as a prisoner in the See-ti.

'It was the only way of getting out of here,' said Pryderi, defending Dryden. 'It was the only plan that might have worked.'

'Well, it did not,' replied Rudhyk. 'The only way out of here is when you die.'

'Not so,' Stigand interposed. 'They say that the *eorl* was about to execute Yaghus when one of the *thegn's* men arrived and ordered him to be taken to *Tún seofen*.'

'Perhaps he was taken there for interrogation,' said one of the men. 'Death - interrogation. It is the same thing.'

'What is more important is the fact that our release from solitary confinement was ordered. The *eorl* of *Tún threo* will not like his judgements changed.'

Pryderi kicked morosely at the floor. If Yaghus was restricted on Level Seven then it was up to Pryderi to effect a rescue - to rescue Yaghus and discover whether his sister Kigva was imprisoned in the See-ti. It was up to him to devise a means of escape now. He sighed deeply. The other men of Hut Six had fallen exhausted onto their bunks. Pryderi moved across to Stigand's bunk and sat on its edge.

'There must be some way to escape,' articulating for the hundredth time the thought that kept hammering in his mind.

'If there was, young man,' returned the elderly Cynn, 'do you think that such a thing would not have been attempted in the generations that the Cynn have kept prisoners? We slaves have lost everything that free men have.'

'The slave loses everything in his bondage, my friend, except the desire to escape from it,' replied Pryderi.

'Fine words, young man,' smiled Stigand. 'But words will not make a force field vanish. The force field binds us more tightly than ropes. Try to break through that field and within a split second you are dead.'

'Nevertheless, no place of bondage has yet been devised by man which man cannot escape from,' said Pryderi.

He was still sitting thinking some hours later. In fact it was nearing the end of the rest period when a smile split the young *drewyth's* face. He bent forward and shook Stigand's arm urgently. The old man woke from his sleep and peered at Pryderi in confusion.

'What is it?'

'No place is escape proof,' he smiled. 'I have just found a way.'

Dryden followed Wulfnoth back through the passageways of Level Seven pondering on the fear and jealousy which he had read in Thaec's face when he looked upon the Faeder Aldgyth. Dimly he remembered something that old Stigand had told him. Thaec was one of the seven most powerful men among the Cynn, the ruler of Level Seven, who hoped to become the next Faeder. How did one dictator take over from another? Surely the answer lay in Thaec's eyes. The days of Aldgyth were obviously numbered - or if Aldgyth knew of the *thegn's* ambitions then the days of Thaec were going to be short.

Wulfnoth turned into the wide corridor which seemed to be a main thoroughfare along which throngs of the Cynn hurried this way and that. It was far more crowded than before. Perhaps it was the end of a work period?

Dryden happened to glance up at one of the buildings which

flanked the thoroughfare. It was more imposing than most he had seen, more ornately structured, and two guards stood outside. As his eyes flickered over its edifice, he caught sight of a figure framed in one of the upstairs windows.

It was the figure of a girl whose hair was of raven blackness, hair which tumbled around a delicate heart-shaped face, whose skin was pale, near white, with just a gentle hint of red across the cheek bones. The mouth was full and naturally red. There was a hint of freckles across the dainty nose. The eyes were grey and sad as they watched the crowd go by.

Dryden froze in his tracks.

'Kigva!' he whispered. Then he cried aloud: 'Kigva!'

The girl looked down - startled, her cheeks reddening.

For a second their eyes met, a joyous expression started to spread across the girl's face and then it seemed someone inside the room, someone whom Dryden could not see, grasped the girl and thrust her swiftly away from the window.

'Kigva!' Dryden turned towards the building but found himself in a vice-like grip. He twisted round at the expressionless face of Wulfnoth and tried to wrest himself free.

'Let me go!' he cried hoarsely in English. 'Let me go ...'

The bald-headed giant held him struggling for a moment and then drew back one balled fist and smacked Dryden on the jaw. Dryden felt something snap and for the second time in a few hours he felt himself diving into a pool of blackness.

Stigand was looking at Pryderi in disbelief.

'How have you been able to devise a plan of escape, young man? I have been here for ten years and have been unable to find even one feasible idea.'

'Sometimes the obvious can be easily overlooked,' grinned Pryderi.

'The obvious?' queried Stigand, watching Pryderi move to the window of the hut.

'On Level One, the level which we are now on, there are two compounds for the slaves. Isn't that so?'

Stigand rose with an affirmative gesture and joined him at the window.

'The two compounds are divided into a compound for male slaves and one for the female slaves. They consist of two large squares. These squares are divided into blocks and there are one hundred blocks in each square. We, for example, are in Block Seventy-Eight.'

Stigand looked impatient.

'I fail to see your point. This much is obvious.'

'One moment. We are in a square divided into blocks, ten blocks in one direction and ten blocks in another direction. It is just like a giant *branvras* board.'

'A what?' asked Stigand, completely lost.

'*Branvras* is a board game that we play in Lan-Kern, a board divided into squares on which counters are moved.'

'So?'

'Now, looking at the compound as if it was a board divided into squares, I have learned that it is divided into three work groups and ten special blocks. The special blocks are on the right hand side of the square and are numbered Block One, Eleven, Twenty-One, Thirty-One and so on up to Ninety-One. The prisoners in those blocks do not work in the culture fields.'

Stigand nodded. 'So far you are right.'

'Very well. The other ninety blocks are divided into three work forces. When a work force is called to go to the elevators for their work period then the force field on those thirty blocks is cut off to allow the prisoners to pass along the pathways to the elevators.'

'Yes,' sighed Stigand. 'But I still don't understand ...'

Pryderi motioned him to silence.

'We are in Block Seventy-Eight.'

'So?'

'When the siren sounds we leave our Block and march dutifully from Block Seventy-Eight into Block Sixty-Eight and then to Fifty-Eight, Forty-Eight and so on to Block Eight which is situated at the perimeter of the compound opposite the elevators.'

Pryderi paused, his eyes alight with excitement.

'Well, isn't it plain?'

Stigand shook his head.

'In Block Seventy-Eight we are only two blocks from the perimeter of the compound in two directions. When the force field is cut off to allow the prisoners to go to the elevator shafts what is to prevent us from running from Block Seventy-Eight to Eighty-Eight and through Ninety-Eight into the area which separates the male compound from the female compound? When the force field is cut off the main perimeter field has to be cut as well to allow the prisoners to move out of the compound.'

'There are guards,' pointed out Stigand.

'We can avoid them,' returned Pryderi. 'Anyway, there is another path of escape - through Block Seventy-Nine and Block Eighty. That would bring us out at the side of the cavern.'

Stigand was dubious, trying not to let himself become infected by Pryderi's eagerness.

'There are patrols all around the perimeter especially when the force field is down.'

'I'd rather take a chance than rot here forever,' replied the young *drewyth.*

Stigand scratched the side of his face.

'It is no use trying to escape through Blocks Eighty-Eight and Ninety-Eight,' he said thoughtfully. 'There are two guard towers there which would spot us immediately.'

Pryderi smiled.

'Then Seventy-Nine and Eighty it is,' he declared, holding out his hand to Stigand. They shook hands silently. Then Pryderi continued. 'As far as I can see, the perimeter fence leads onto an area of twenty yards of empty space before the walls of the cavern. From what I have seen, the cavern walls are rough and could provide us with some sort of shelter while we consider our next step.'

Stigand smiled.

'I think we are being foolish. It has never been done before and yet it seems too simple not to have been considered.'

'Perhaps that is why no one has tried it before?' suggested Pryderi. 'People are often confused by simplicity.'

'When shall we make the attempt?'

'As soon as the siren sounds.'

Already the warning wail of the breakfast siren was starting its drone.

'Let's get some food in our bellies first,' said Stigand.

A short time later the main siren sounded. Dutifully, the prisoners of Block Seventy-Eight began to line up and move off in the direction of the elevators. Stigand and Pryderi hung back until the contingents from Block Eighty-Eight and Ninety-Eight passed through their section followed by a nonchalant guard. No guard bothered to look in the huts, no prisoner dared to hide from the work call for they were counted as they moved to the elevators. That left Pryderi and Stigand only a few moments to effect their escape.

'Now!' snapped Pryderi, moving swiftly from the hut.

Heart in mouth he jumped across the small boundary wire into the neighbouring Block Seventy-Nine, his skin itching, half expecting to feel the terrible shock of the force field. But no shock came. The force field was down as he knew it would be.

'Again!' he cried, as Stigand followed him across Block Seventy-Nine and over the perimeter wire into Block Eighty. Only twenty yards away now the stone walls of the great cavern rose towering over the compound.

'Keep going for the perimeter,' Pryderi called to Stigand who was gasping for breath as he ran close behind.

The border fence was three feet high and designed only to mark the boundaries of the compound because the force field did all the work of constraining the inmates of the various blocks. Pryderi was just about to climb over when he halted, turned and drew Stigand back into the shelter of a nearby hut.

'A patrol.'

They watched dry mouthed as the three black uniformed guards marched slowly past.

'We can't wait much longer,' whispered Stigand. 'The force field will come on any time now.'

Pryderi nodded.

'We must go now,' he said.

'But the guards will see us,' protested the old man.

'Now!' insisted Pryderi, running towards the fence.

The guards were thirty yards away with their backs turned. Pryderi seized the top of the fence with both hands and vaulted over. He turned to see Stigand gazing uncertainly at the obstacle and waved him impatiently forward. Biting his lip, Stigand hauled himself over the fence and fell at Pryderi's feet.

'Quickly,' cried the young man, hauling Stigand to his feet.

There was a sudden buzzing in the air. The force field had been switched on. Stigand looked sick. Another few seconds and...

'Come on!'

They had covered ten of the twenty yards that separated them from the shadowy cavern wall when a harsh cry cracked across the area.

'Healt!'

Pryderi froze but it was a pause of a split second and then he was half pushing, half dragging Stigand with him towards the cavern walls. There came a faint explosion behind him and he felt a surge of hot air rush by his cheek. Then they were against the rough hewn walls of the cavern where rubble and some fallen stone provided cover. Both men flung themselves down as two more shots blasted the air above them.

'We must find better shelter than this,' gasped Pryderi.

Stigand could not reply but he pointed further along the cavern walls.

'Can you make it?' demanded Pryderi.

The old man nodded.

'Forbidden Zone...along there...small cave leads off...shelter...'

Crouching low, with Pryderi leading the way, the two dodged through the rubble. Behind them came further shouting and shooting. A great whining siren filled the air with its clamour - the alarm from the compound announcing their escape. Abruptly Pryderi came to a small aperture in the cavern wall scarcely big enough for a man to squeeze through. There was a board next to it which had one word written on it: *'Forbéodan.'* He turned to Stigand.

'Yes, that's it,' cried the old man. 'Quickly. It's the Forbidden Zone, we'll be safe there.'

Pryderi squeezed through into a small black passage. He felt Stigand press close behind him.

'I cannot see,' complained Pryderi.

A sudden beam of light lit the small passage before him.

'Here - there are some torches by the entrance,' said Stigand, breathlessly. 'Take these two. We'll use one at a time. I'll take two more.'

Pryderi looked in amazement at the torch and then dismissed it. Already in the See-ti he had seen too many marvellous inventions for them to seem miracles any more. And there was no time to meditate on such things.

'Where to?' he asked.

'As far as we can go through the passage,' returned Stigand. 'The further we go in the better. They will not follow us here.'

Pryderi did not ask why. He trusted Stigand's knowledge.

Outside, the *weardian* Mandubert halted his men and shook his head slowly.

'What shall we do now?' demanded one of the guards.

Mandubert hunched his shoulders.

'They have gone into the Forbidden Zone. What can we do?'

The guard was young and enthusiastic.

'Can't we follow?'

Mandubert laughed hollowly.

'Follow? Into the Forbidden Zone? Listen, *boi*...'

The guard reddened. He was young enough to dislike being called 'boy'.

'Listen, in a few hours they will be dead anyway. No one returns from the Forbidden Zone. Let's go and report to the *eorl* Gréne.'

CHAPTER FOUR

The face of Thaec was staring coldly down at him when Dryden opened his eyes.

'You should not have attempted to escape,' rebuked the *thegn* of Level Seven. 'Wulfnoth would not have hit you.'

Dryden shook his head groggily and tried to sit up. He was back in the room with the golden lights. Memories raced through his befuddled mind and he started up.

'Kigva!'

Thaec gazed at him bewildered.

'What?'

Dryden tried to piece his shattered thoughts together.

'I was not trying to escape. I saw someone - someone I know. I wanted to speak to her.'

Thaec frowned.

'Someone named Kigva?'

'Yes.'

'That's an outlander name - a female name. You saw an outlander here on Level Seven?' Suspicion edged the *thegn's* voice.

Dryden felt he had nothing to lose in admitting Kigva's presence on Level Seven. It was obvious from his expression that Thaec did not know of her. But perhaps Thaec could lead him to Kigva. The *thegn* turned to Wulfnoth, who stood behind him, and spoke to him curtly. The man responded rapidly, pointing once or twice to Dryden. A grim smile began to form around Thaec's mouth.

'*Swá*?' he breathed gently. 'The residence to which you seemed so intent on going is the private residence of our Faeder. Just what would your outlander friend be doing there do you think?'

Dryden bit his lip in anguish. He could hazard a guess.

'Perhaps, Dryden, you'd better tell me who this girl Kigva is.'

Dryden explained briefly how he and Pryderi had followed

91

Kigva through the forests in order to bring her safely back to Lan-Kern.

'And what is this Kigva to you?' asked Thaec.

Dryden hesitated.

'Ha!' barked the *thegn.* 'You need say no more, outlander.'

He turned and drummed his fingers on his forehead.

'You have set us a problem, outlander. I will see to it that enquiries are made at the residence of the Faeder. It is interesting that he is holding a girl of inferior breed in his residency.'

'I hold no human to be inferior to another,' snapped Dryden.

Thaec grinned.

'Ah? Gréne said you were a man of scruples - well, when we have talked some more perhaps we shall overcome them for you.'

'What of Kigva?' demanded Dryden.

Thaec held up his hand.

'Leave it to me to make enquiries. You cannot openly demand information from the Faeder. He is...' Thaec paused and his mouth drooped cynically, 'all powerful. We will find out what has been happening. In the meantime there is to be a review of our foremost warriors, men who will soon sweep across the world and reclaim it for the Cynn.'

Thaec's eyes sparkled with a sudden flash of fanaticism. It was gone again in a moment. Dryden began to realise that Thaec was a dangerous zealot who fully believed in the crusade of the Cynn to dominate the world. He saw that he would have to humour this man, for he was the only Cynn leader who had attempted to form some relationship with him and perhaps through that relationship, weakness could be discovered.

'May I watch this review of your army?' he asked, trying to shut Kigva out of his mind.

'The whole nation of the Cynn is an army,' returned Thaec. 'They are trained, disciplined and ready for the most glorious moment in their history. In a short while the Faeder will review the *Tún seofen* battle formations and speak to them of the great purpose of the Cynn which they will soon fulfil. Wulfnoth will conduct you to a place where you may watch. But now I must change into my ceremonial uniform.'

Thaec turned towards the door.

'And you will make enquiries about Kigva?' asked Dryden anxiously.

Thaec half turned and smiled.

'Never fear upon that matter, outlander.'

Pryderi paused for a moment and shone a beam of light in Stigand's direction.

'You'd better rest awhile,' he said. 'I don't think the guards are following us.'

Stigand gratefully sank to the floor of the passageway.

'No,' he gasped, 'they wouldn't follow us into the Forbidden Zone.'

Pryderi began to examine the smooth passageway.

'Why is it called the Forbidden Zone and why wouldn't people come in here?'

Stigand drew several breaths to regulate his breathing.

'The Forbidden Zone has always been the Forbidden Zone ever since our earliest records - perhaps even as far back as the building of the See-ti. Those few people who have dared to venture inside have never come back.'

Pryderi looked at the old man.

'Yet you led us in here,' he pointed out.

Stigand peered round with a shudder.

'We are dead one way or another, Pryderi,' he said simply.

'Are you ready to go on?' asked Pryderi, dismissing the subject.

'Go on?' Stigand seemed amazed.

'We can't go back,' Pryderi explained patiently. 'It is obvious that this passage was built for a purpose. It must lead somewhere. Therefore, old friend, we will follow it. Perhaps it will lead us out of the See-ti.'

'But it is the Forbidden Zone,' protested Stigand.

'As you said, if we go back we are dead, so why not go forward?'

Pryderi shone his torch around the tunnel walls. Certainly, judging by their smoothness, they were man-made and ropes of some kind of spongy substance ran along one side of the tunnel wall. Above them were some strange hieroglyphics which Pryderi asked Stigand to decipher. Stigand gazed at them and finally told him that they were not written in the language of the Cynn although, he added, there seemed a degree of similarity.

Having rested, Stigand announced that he felt able to continue and Pryderi set off up the tunnel which began to twist and spiral upwards.

'Perhaps it leads to the surface?' suggested Pryderi in excitement.

'It is the Forbidden Zone,' muttered Stigand, glancing anxiously about.

They came abruptly to a vault-like chamber. It was full of strange objects, the like of which Pryderi had never seen before. It smelled musty and thick dust lay everywhere. He swung his torch across the chamber.

It was Stigand who gave a cry of alarm as the torch fell on what seemed to be a group of silent, standing figures.

Pryderi let out a soft exclamation and moved closer. They were not human figures, but strange suits suspended on wires. They seemed to be made of one piece of material, stretching from boots to large bulb-shaped helmets which were attached to the neck of the suit. A visor of some dark glass-like substance completely covered the front of the helmet.

'These are strange garments,' muttered the young *drewyth*. 'Perhaps they are for some special purpose?'

'I have no knowledge of this place,' replied Stigand, his voice trembling.

Wiping aside the dust and dirt, Pryderi discovered that the chamber was lined with banks of control instruments, with gauges and dials, fairly similar to the control areas of the various levels. Several short tunnels led off from the chamber but, to Pryderi's disappointment, most of them ended within a few yards. One of them was a large recess which seemed to end in a wall of smooth metal. On this metal were several more strange hieroglyphics. It was to examine these characters that Pryderi stepped into the recess.

What happened then was totally unexpected.

A red light switched on in a side wall and there came a strange, humming noise.

Pryderi stepped back abruptly and the red light went out and the noise ceased.

'*Aelmihtig!*' exclaimed Stigand, cowering back.

Pryderi frowned. He moved forward again. The red light came

on and the noise sounded again.

He turned to Stigand.

'My body must activate some control here - it is the same as when you pass through a door in the See-ti and they open without you pushing them.'

Stigand moved forward reluctantly, trying to overcome his nerves. He was obviously still in awe of the Forbidden Zone. Pryderi moved further into the recess in order to examine the metal wall at the back of it. Stigand was looking around, a little less fearful than before.

'Why,' his voice became animated. 'I do believe that this is the entrance to an elevator. Do you see that small patch of glass to your left? Well, pass your hand over it.'

Pryderi did so and sprang back as the smooth metal wall slid aside revealing a small square room beyond. For a moment he stood examining it in the light of his torch. Like everything else it was coated with dust. He turned to Stigand.

'A way out?'

Stigand moved forward with some reluctance.

'Who knows where it will lead?'

'There is only one way to find out,' declared Pryderi, stepping into the lift and motioning Stigand to follow.

'How is it operated?'

'Pass your hand over the glass panel there,' pointed Stigand.

The doors slid shut. The air inside was foul.

'And now?'

The light of their torch revealed a series of buttons. There were no indications.

'Try one of those,' instructed Stigand. 'We are in the lap of the *Aelmihtig*.'

Pryderi jabbed at the top button.

There was a whirring noise and a faint jar which sent Pryderi colliding into Stigand so that they both fell against the side of the elevator. For some moments Pryderi felt dizzy as the lift accelerated but whether it was going upwards or downwards he had no way of telling.

Abruptly there came a feeling of sickness, his stomach seemed to leap into his mouth, as the lift decelerated and came to a halt. He looked at Stigand, his face pale in the torchlight.

'Pass your hand over the panel to open the doors,' the old man said in a voice hoarse with expectancy.

Pryderi did so.

The doors seemed to slide back very slowly.

Pryderi took a hesitant step forward and shone his torch around. At once he felt an overwhelming sense of disappointment.

'The lift could not have moved,' he whispered. The chamber reflected in the light from his beam was exactly the same as the one from which they had come.

It was Stigand who pointed out the difference.

'Look! We are in a different chamber.'

Pryderi shone his torch in the direction of the trembling finger of the old man and found that certain details differed. Where the other chamber had been dusty, this one was strewn with musty, dank smelling earth. And he became aware of a curious light in the chamber.

'Bel be praised!' cried Pryderi, pointing to the roof of the chamber. In one corner there seemed to be a small patch of light which cast a glow through the room. 'We are on the surface!'

'The surface?' exclaimed Stigand in astonishment.

Pryderi was already on the far side of the chamber, scrambling up towards a hole through which earth and rock cascaded as he tried to pull himself upwards.

'Come on, Stigand! I need your help,' he called impatiently.

'It is dark there, are you sure that is the surface?'

'It is night-time, Stigand - I see a star-speckled night sky, a beautiful sky and a rising moon.' He suddenly stopped. Of course most of the people of the See-ti had never been to the surface in their lives and would not understand the natural phenomena of day and night. He began to explain but Stigand interrupted.

'I know the concepts, Pryderi. Indeed, I have been on the surface, but only in the daylight. You see, all the Cynn prisoners were used for experimentation in tolerance of the surface light. I was one of the lucky ones who did not go blind. I seem to have an immunity to it.'

With Stigand's help, Pryderi climbed his way through the hole which had been created by a cave-in of the roof of the chamber. It was a tiny hole but Pryderi managed, albeit with some difficulty, to gain the surface and lie panting up at the clear night sky. After a time he leaned into the hole and reached down towards Stigand. 'Give me your hand and I'll haul you up.' The old man clasped the outstretched hand and within moments lay on the grass beside him.

Almost at once the old man moaned and clutched at the young *drewyth*.

'*Aelmihtig*! The sky ... it is so large ... I never dreamed ... so huge ... so empty!'

'I thought you had been to the surface?'

'But in daylight only. The night sky - with its myriad stars - makes it seem so vast compared with daylight.'

Stigand breathed heavily and slowly relaxed his clutching hold on Pryderi. 'Do not mind me now, it was a moment of panic. This space, this emptiness, will take a little getting used to.'

Seeing the old man had recovered, Pryderi stood up and examined his surroundings with interest. They appeared to be in a copse of tall conifers set at the edge of a vast plain of waving grass. The moon was full, just above the horizon, and casting a broad pale light on the scene. Pryderi suddenly tensed and pointed.

'A fire!' he whispered. Through the trees came a flickering yellow light. 'Cynn?'

'Our people do not stay on the surface at night,' replied Stigand, with a shake of his head.

'Follow me closely then and do not speak,' instructed Pryderi.

Half crouching, the young man edged forward through the trees towards the light. Stigand followed blindly behind, trying to avert his eyes from the terrible open canopy of sky above him.

From the cover of some bushes Pryderi gazed upon a small camp fire. A woman - no, a young girl was cooking something in a pot. Even in this light Pryderi could see her blonde attractiveness. A man was squatting with his back towards Pryderi's watching eyes. The woman said something and the man laughed heartily. Pryderi took in their costume. Well, one thing was certain - they were not of the See-ti.

Slowly he rose to his feet and, with Stigand behind him, he moved forward a few paces out of the bushes. The girl at the fire looked up with a cry of startled alarm and the man turned in one fleet, crouching movement. As if by magic a length of glinting, sharp steel appeared as an extension of his hand and the blade of the sword was at Pryderi's throat.

Pryderi stepped backwards, his face drawing into a mask of dismay and then hatred.

'Cador!' he breathed.

CHAPTER FIVE

Dryden found himself in a big square in the middle of Level Seven. It was so massive that his breath was taken away momentarily. White buildings with balconies crowded with people rose on all sides of the square which had the appearance of a good sized stadium. At one end of it was a dais to which the surly Wulfnoth conducted him. On it were about twenty or more people, men and women, all in the ominous uniforms of the Cynn. As Wulfnoth led him forward the *thegn* Thaec, resplendent in a white uniform, smiled thinly.

'Well, outlander, I trust you appreciate the honour done you?'

'Honour?' Dryden was curious.

'You are the first outlander to be allowed to attend a review by the Faeder.'

The others on the platform were examining Dryden with disdainful glances. Thaec turned and went to the forefront of the dais while Wulfnoth motioned Dryden to a position at the back. All around were large flags bearing the red cross against a white background. The people on the platform were obviously of importance, perhaps *eorls* or even *thegns*, each with uniforms bearing badges of rank which meant nothing to Dryden.

Before long there came a soft murmuring and then a single trumpet sounded. The lean figure of Aldgyth, Faeder of the Cynn, strode forward from a nearby building, flanked by several guards. He was dressed entirely in white and gold. Everyone stiffened to attention as he climbed onto the dais. Then another trumpet sounded and from the far side of the square Dryden saw a line of marching figures entering between the buildings. Thousands of Cynn marched into the square, all clad in black uniforms, all stamping in unison. They spread like some black tide swiftly across the parade ground. Their stamping feet echoed to the rhythmic sound of a drum.

Dryden watched as they marched, counter-marched and drilled. He had a kind of admiration for their discipline; an admiration for their co-ordination and manoeuvring. At the same time he felt fear of the military power they symbolised, the power of death and destruction, as they stamped their feet to the banging of the drum. The drum! The man who gave soldiers a drum must have known what he was doing for the drum drove out all thought with its hypnotic beat. He looked hard at the marching mass and shook his head sorrowfully as he realised that the admiration he had for their discipline was no more than the admiration he would have for any trained, performing animal. Sometimes it was hard to see the truth when you saw soldiers clad in smart uniforms and drilling with superb ease; sometimes you forgot they were merely a mob and like mobs they react *en masse* and lose their individuality and humanity; that they fought only with a courage borrowed from their mass and not with the courage of an individual facing danger. Mobs were such pitiful things. He smiled cynically when he recalled some lines from Homer's *Iliad*:

Our business in the field of fight

Is not to question, but to prove our might.

And this was what the Cynn held to be civilisation? Rather this was the very essence of primitivism.

He was aware of an abrupt silence. A single note from the trumpet had caused the marching men to crash to a halt as one person. There were several seconds of a silence so complete that Dryden imagined he could hear his heart beat. Then, with an ear-splitting loudness, single voiced the entire company shouted: '*Heill Faeder! Heill! Heill! Heill!*'

It sent a shiver down Dryden's back.

Aldgyth stepped forward, hands on hips, and for a moment stared at the warriors before him. He began to speak, slowly at first, clearly articulating each word. Then his voice became excited, his figure more animated and the words started tumbling over each other until his voice rose to a crescendo, at which point he paused for breath. Whatever he had said, the Cynn roared their approval. It reminded Dryden of something he had seen in his youth - and he felt sickened.

Then the troops were marching away; Aldgyth had disappeared

from the dais and Thaec was standing regarding him in amusement.

'Well, outlander? Were you not impressed by the might and discipline of the Cynn! In a few weeks' time our armies will erupt over the earth to reclaim the birthright that is ours. Are we not invincible?'

Pryderi gazed on the former war-lord of Lan-Howlek in defiance. 'Well, Cador of Lan-Howlek,' he sneered. 'Why don't you slay me as you slew my brother Peredur?'

But Cador dropped his sword and stared at Pryderi in bewilderment.

'Cador?' he asked hesitantly. 'Why do you call me Cador ...? My name is... Cad.'

Pryderi frowned.

'What game is this, Cador?'

The girl, Onnen, came forward slowly, her face pale even in the glow of the firelight.

'You say you know this man?' she whispered, directing her question at Pryderi.

The young *drewyth* nodded, his eyes darting from Cador to the girl.

'And who do you say he is?' pressed the girl.

'He is Cador, grandson of Nelferch, the deposed tyrant ruler of Lan-Howlek.'

Cador looked thunderstruck.

The girl swayed a little and made an effort to control herself.

'I swear I remember nothing of this ...' began Cador.

'You are sure that he is Cador? You can positively identify him as such?' persisted the girl.

'I can,' replied Pryderi shortly.

'But you said that I told you my name was Cad before I was knocked unconscious,' said Cador to the girl. There was no mistaking the genuine look of bafflement on his face.

Onnen nodded. 'That is what you told me. Small wonder if you are Cador of Lan-Howlek.'

'What is this?' asked Pryderi.

'He has lost his memory. An *ors* attacked him and knocked him unconscious and since then he has remembered nothing prior to that time.' She paused. 'Who are you, stranger?'

'I am Pryderi, son of Kesmur, ruler of Lan-Kern.'

'And the old one?' The girl pointed to Stigand who stood perplexed.

'That is Stigand of the Cynn, an inhabitant of the See-ti. We have just escaped together.'

The girl nodded thoughtfully, still concerned with Pryderi's revelation.

'I have heard of you, Pryderi of Lan-Kern. I am named Onnen, I am from the northern lands of Lan-Howlek. You mentioned that Nelferch has been deposed. How do you know this? Is it true?'

'It is true. I was there. The people' rose up and overthrew her. Cador escaped from Dynas Drok, taking with him *An Kevryn*, the great symbol of creation, which he had originally stolen from the sanctuary at Meneghy. I and another, my friend Yaghus, pursued him to recover it. Also, a short time before he fled, my sister Kigva, who had been his prisoner, escaped and fled into the eastern forests. Cador was pursuing her and we were pursuing him.'

'Kigva!' Cador dropped his sword and raised his hands to his forehead.

Onnen had paled considerably. 'That is the name of her whom he was following.'

'I thought he could not recall anything?' questioned Pryderi.

'Before the *ors* attacked,' explained Onnen, 'he rescued me from the *morlader* and the men of the See-ti and told me his name was Cad and that he was searching for someone called Kigva. That and no more.'

Cador was groaning slightly.

'I cannot remember. What nightmare is this? Who am I? What am I?'

Onnen was clearly moved by the tortured features of the man she had grown to love as Cad. Her heart suddenly went out to him in spite of the bitter shock at his identification. She reached forward and laid a hand on his arm.

'Whatever you were, Cador of Lan-Howlek, you are not the same man now.'

Cador grasped her hand.

'Was this man Cador truly bad?'

She bit her lip.

'Perhaps not all ...'

Pryderi interrupted, not being able to relate to the new circumstances, demanding an explanation. Onnen related in detail her meeting with Cador. The young *drewyth* gazed with scepticism at the man.

'And Kigva? And *An Kevryn*? You recall nothing of them?'

Cador shook his head.

'I knew that I was following someone called Kigva and she, I hoped, would tell me who I was. But as for the rest, I know nothing. I do not know what manner of man I was. You say I am Nelferch's grandson? But Onnen has told me that she was evil, that her grandson was a despot. Am I that man?'

Once again Onnen laid a pacifying hand on Cador's arm.

'It is the man you are now that matters. If the memory returns and you recall your past life, then so be it. If not, live as you want to do now, not in the past.'

She shot a defiant look at Pryderi.

'And you, Pryderi of Lan-Kern, do you seek vengeance?'

Vengeance? Pryderi looked at the bewildered pain-racked face of his former enemy. Vengeance? Justice? The man had no recall of his past. He let out a deep sigh.

'Be in peace, Onnen. Before I was forced to take up the sword to defend my people from the attacks of Nelferch I was a *drewyth*, trained in the ways of peace. In peace I now say let this matter take a natural course. What is the point of accusations against a man who does not remember his crimes? In such a case crime and punishment are flowers on the same bush.'

Onnen smiled gently.

'Spoken in a true knowledge of the purpose of Bel.'

She turned to Cador and took both of his hands in hers.

'I grew to hate Cador of Lan-Howlek by tales of his deeds, by his evil reputation. In the past week I have grown to love the man called Cad. Nothing he has done since I have known him has changed that love.'

'But if I am the man he says I am, and that man was an evil man ...'

'Let time resolve the matter as time surely will.'

103

Cador lowered his head.

'I pray time will return my memory.'

They sat uncomfortably around the fire and Onnen, seeing how exhausted Pryderi and Stigand really were, fussed over the fire where she was preparing *gourgath* steaks. As they ate, Stigand doing so with some surprise, having eaten yeast-based foods all his life, Pryderi told their story.

'We think that Kigva may be held in Level Seven where my friend Yaghus was taken.'

Onnen was shaking her head in amazement.

'And, you say, this See-ti is a vast underground settlement?'

'Built many centuries ago, my child, on seven levels thousands of feet below the surface of the earth,' replied Stigand. 'Thus it was thought, during the Great Destruction, that the élite of the human race would be sheltered and spared to recreate the world.'

'And,' went on Onnen, 'you also say that the Cynn are soon to attack Lan-Howlek and Lan-Kern?'

Stigand shrugged: 'The Cynn are invincible. I know, for I was one of the Cynn until I started to doubt the morality of the Faeder's purpose.'

'It will be difficult to stop the Cynn, I agree,' said Pryderi. 'They have a technology that seems magical to us.'

'Nevertheless, what chance have our people of survival if such an evil is not fought?' demanded Onnen.

'If only your friend Yaghus was here to advise us,' sighed Stigand. 'He had a mind that refused to accept defeat.'

'Yaghus!' the word was a long, drawn out sigh.

They turned to look at Cador who was frowning into the flames of the camp fire.

'The name means something to you, Cad - Cador?' queried Onnen softly.

'Yes - for a moment. Now it is gone.' He sighed.

'Where is this Yaghus now?' asked Onnen.

'A prisoner on Level Seven.'

'It seems to me,' said Pryderi slowly, 'that our first task is to devise a way to rescue Yaghus and Kigva, if she is a prisoner of the Cynn.'

'How?' asked Onnen. 'If the See-ti lies beneath the surface, how can we get down there?'

Pryderi smiled. 'The same way that we escaped. We have discovered a disused entrance.'

'But it only leads to the Forbidden Zone of Level One,' protested Stigand.

'You remember all the buttons in the elevator?' returned Pryderi. 'It is my belief that it was designed to descend or ascend to each level and if we press the eighth button on the panel we shall emerge on the Seventh Level.'

'Then what?' demanded Stigand. 'Can you fight the whole Cynn by yourselves? Wouldn't it be better to flee back to your own country to prepare them against the Cynn invasion?'

'No!' snapped Pryderi. 'I will not leave this place until we have rescued my sister Kigva and my friend Yaghus.'

Onnen looked at Cador. He was poking the fire morosely with a stick.

'I shall come with you, Pryderi of Lan-Kern,' he suddenly said. 'I have no remembrance of my former life but if, as you say, the girl Kigva was captured by the Cynn because of my actions, then my moral duty is clear. Also this man Yaghus, whose name seems so familiar to me, is a prisoner in the See-ti because of my deeds. I will join you, Pryderi, if you will have me as a companion in the venture.'

Onnen smiled broadly.

'Where Cad - Cador - goes, I will go too. So there are three of us.'

'Four,' added Stigand. 'I might as well join you in your folly for you will need someone who knows the ways of the Cynn and their language.'

'Very well. I suggest we sleep now and at dawn we'll try to make our way down to Level Seven.'

'And if we reach Level Seven - what then?' asked Stigand.

'We'll let the fates decide.'

CHAPTER SIX

Dryden sat in the chair to which Thaec motioned him and asked: 'Have you any news of Kigva?'

The *thegn* of Level Seven shook his head.

'I can confirm that she is being held in the apartments of the Faeder and at his especial orders. She has apparently been there since she was captured. More than that, outlander, I do not know. My men are making enquiries.'

Dryden peered into the bland face of Thaec and fought down a desire to rush from the room to the Faeder's apartments.

'You have no idea why Kigva is being held here, on Level Seven?'

Thaec waved a hand, dismissively.

'We shall soon know, do not worry, outlander. In the meantime I want to talk to you about joining the Cynn in their great enterprise.'

Dryden sighed. He must be careful with the man if he was to get anywhere in an attempt to rescue Kigva.

'The *eorl* Gréne said you had scruples,' Thaec said mildly. 'In spite of what he says I believe you have let your personal dislike of Gréne discolour your view of our society and its purpose.'

'You wish to conquer the world,' Dryden blurted out. 'That is a simple concept to grasp.'

'It is our destiny, our duty, to conquer the world.' Thaec's eyes blazed suddenly as he leaned forward in his chair.

Dryden did not reply. He told himself once again to guard his tongue and be careful with this man. Thaec was leaning back in his chair and smiling, almost apologetically.

'You see, Dryden, you are not of the Cynn. And yet, if the story that you and Gréne tell of coming from an age before the Great Destruction is true, then you are the remote ancestors of the Cynn. Surely, therefore, you can appreciate the purpose of the Cynn?'

'I can see little purpose in conquest,' said Dryden, choosing his

106

words carefully. 'What purpose is there in waging a terrible warfare on a people because you claim they are inferior breeds? Surely, they could claim as much about the Cynn? Neither is inferior - only different.'

Thaec shook his head slowly.

'When we go forth upon the surface we will be fighting for the loftiest and most overpowering purpose that man can conceive - it will be for the freedom and independence of our race, the security of our future food supplies and our racial honour.'

Again Dryden caught the fanatical gleam in the man's eye, the earnest belief of the zealot, the attitude that would abide no dissension.

'The surface is large and sparsely populated,' Dryden felt compelled to point out. 'If you want to leave the See-ti and go out to live on the surface, then why can't you co-exist with the other peoples of the world? There is room enough for all.'

'Co-exist with inferior breeds, breeds which might act as a pollutant to our racial purity?' Thaec laughed.

'Why do you consider the surface dwellers are inferior?' pressed Dryden.

'Simple,' returned Thaec. 'Humanity is divided into three classes. There are the founders of civilisation, the upholders of civilisation and the destroyers of civilisation. It was our ancient forebears who built the See-ti at the time of the Great Destruction. They founded our civilisation. We, the Cynn, living as our ancestors so ordained, are the upholders of that civilisation. The destroyers are those who are alien to our civilisation. They are the destroyers because, being alien and not capable of understanding, they would contaminate it and eventually tear it down. The existence of survivors on the surface was initially considered by our learned men to be a mistake of nature. However, nature makes no mistakes for there is a purpose in all things.'

'Now that I can agree with,' nodded Dryden. 'But what purpose do *you* see in the survival of the surface dwellers?'

'Lesser breeds are a prerequisite for the re-establishment of civilisation upon the earth's surface.'

'Don't you concede that the surface dwellers have their own civilisation, just as valid although not a technically advanced?'

'Nonsense! Only the Cynn are possessed of the true morals, technology and purpose which make a truly civilised people.'

'The Cynn are therefore superior?' queried Dryden, trying to grasp the philosophy which spurred the people of the See-ti.

'Is there any question of that?' demanded Thaec. 'The Cynn were ordained by the highest intellects, at the time of the Great Destruction, to seek shelter in the bowels of the earth in order to survive the catastrophe and then come forth to breed anew, to inherit the world as their own. Only the Cynn were so ordained as the people who were physically and mentally perfected to rebuild the world and establish a new order of society.

'The indissoluble unity of blood, the purity of the Cynn, is indispensable for the health of the Cynn. Any dilution by intermarriage with the inferior breeds who survived on the surface - those who have been subjected to the ravages of diseases and plagues during the Great Destruction - would weaken and destroy us - physically, morally and culturally.'

'Then why do you say that the surface dwellers are a prerequisite for the re-establishment of your civilisation?' asked Dryden. 'I thought it was a Cynn teaching that the inferior breeds were to be annihilated - destroyed?'

Thaec nodded

'So it is - eventually. But man's first civilisation rested upon the use of inferior races. Those whose civilisation had developed discipline and weaponry soon conquered those who were less advanced. According to our ancient records on pre-history, the vanquished races pulled the plough and tended the fields while the conquerors went forth to increase their influence. The lesser breeds, therefore, played their part in freeing the conquering race from the economic chores of society. The Cynn are merely fulfilling the great irrevocable law of Nature.'

Thaec drummed a tattoo on the arm of his chair with his fingers.

'I will confess to you, Dryden, that our great purpose was lost sight of over many generations of dwelling within the See-ti; lost sight of until intrepid explorers went forth once more to look upon the surface of the world. It was then, under the greatest of our Faeders, Ulfketul, that the purpose and destiny of the Cynn became clear once again. It was Ulfketul who shaped our will and purpose.'

Dryden choked back his thoughts to ask:

'And it will be the Faeder Aldgyth who will lead the Cynn on their mission of conquest?'

For a moment anger creased Thaec's face.

'Aldgyth?' His voice betrayed utter contempt. Then, it seemed to Dryden, Thaec fought for and won control of his emotions. But in that split second Dryden realised the intensity of Thaec's ambition to become Faeder.

Silently, Dryden wondered what fate Thaec had in store for Aldgyth. He was not concerned at Aldgyth's fate for it seemed that the man was as tyrannical as Thaec. They were two dogs fighting for the possession of a bone, each driven by a fanatical lust for power.

'But you, Thaec - surely you have a great part to play in this?' Dryden pressed again.

Thaec nodded solemnly, his mind elsewhere.

'I follow my course with the precision and security of a sleepwalker.'

The door slid back and Wulfnoth entered and whispered urgently to the *thegn* who replied and turned a bland face to Dryden.

'You may rest awhile here. I shall return to tell you news of the girl, Kigva, soon.'

He left with Wulfnoth.

Dryden sat for some moments with his thoughts whirling. Nelferch had sought power and domination in Lan-Howlek knowing her intentions to be wrong but justifying them with the theory that 'might created right'. Yet in the society of the Cynn evil was considered to be a virtue and a purpose. He shuddered. He must rescue Kigva and Pryderi. And he must find a way of stopping the Cynn from achieving their purpose. But how? How could the people of Lan-Kern and Lan-Howlek stop the Cynn, swords against guns, horses against helicopters, the bravery of individual warriors against a disciplined army? *He had to escape*!

He began to look around the room, his mind working feverishly. It was no good trying to seek an exit through the door. Wulfnoth would probably be on guard outside or, if not Wulfnoth, then some of the black uniformed *weardian*.

The room was square with smooth white walls and ceiling. A couch stood against one corner and some cupboards stood in another.

There were chairs and a table. Just by the cupboards, at floor level, something which looked like an air conditioner duct, some two feet wide and about eighteen inches in height, opened into the wall. He bent down to examine it and felt the soft movement of air against his face.

To his surprise he found that the grille unlatched easily from the wall and he peered through the tunnel. It seemed to stretch only a distance of six feet before emerging into another room. Dryden did not pause to consider the consequences but plunged head first into the aperture, narrow as it was. He pushed himself along and, within a few moments, he had detached the second grille and wriggled through into a large and comfortably furnished room. It was full of rich drapes and had several alcoves in which soft lights played and gave an impression of utter luxury. He realised that this was some sort of sleeping chamber.

He turned and replaced the grille and began to make his way towards the door. He had reached out an arm to investigate its opening mechanism, as it had not slid automatically open as he neared it like most of the other See-ti doors did, when he heard a sound outside. He hurriedly recrossed the room and pressed back into the shadows of an alcove, taking a stand behind a drape.

Thaec and Green entered the room. They were talking rapidly in the language of the Cynn. Green's face was animated but Thaec's face was calm and unperturbed. Suddenly Thaec glanced round suspiciously and for a moment Dryden thought he had been detected. The *thegn* held up a hand and, to Dryden's astonishment, exclaimed in English:

'Let us make use of the outlander tongue which you have taught me. The Faeder has spies everywhere and it is best no man of the Cynn may understand our words.'

Green nodded. 'I tell you, Thaec, it is a dangerous plan. What if it does not succeed? It depends so much on the man's reactions.'

'Does not succeed?' There was scorn in Thaec's voice. 'Rather you should say what if the atmosphere controls of the Cynn fail or the water tanks cease to function properly. No, my friend, Aldgyth will be assassinated - he will be killed by the outlander, Dryden. The Cynn will rise up in anger. The outlander will be slain. Then I shall be swept to power as the new Faeder and I will pledge myself to the conquest of all outlanders. We shall then go forth and conquer this miserable world.'

Dryden was numb with shock. Aldgyth was to die. He had suspected as much. But Thaec was planning that the Faeder of the Cynn should die by his hand. How?

'But it rests on the degree of feeling he has for this girl ... what was her name?'

'Kigva.' Thaec smiled. 'My friend, do not worry on that account. My instinct enables me to feel the most secret desires, the least permissible instincts, sufferings and ambitions. Dryden is in love with the girl. He will kill for her. And I have arranged it so.'

The door suddenly swept back and Wulfnoth stood hesitantly on the threshold.

'*Mín thegn*,' he bowed. '*Mín thegn, the útlander*...' Whatever he said, Dryden realised that Wulfnoth had discovered his absence from the room but could not have spotted the open grille for Thaec, with a stifled exclamation, sprang to his feet, followed by Green, and went muttering from the room.

CHAPTER SEVEN

Pryderi pressed the release mechanism for the door of the elevator.

'If my guess is right,' he declared, as Stigand, Cador and Onnen peered over his shoulder while the door slid open, 'this should be Level Seven.'

The chamber in which the elevator stood was dark, the air dank and stale.

'It's like the other chambers,' whispered Stigand, peering round at the dust covered banks of instruments which covered the walls of the chamber.

Onnen gave a stifled scream and pointed. It seemed that a line of half-a-dozen shadowy figures stood close by a wall but Pryderi, shining the beam of his torch on them, soon discovered they were but a row of strange and empty suits similar to those he had found on Level One. Again he wondered what their purpose had been, for they seemed so strange and cumbersome.

Two passageways led from the chamber.

'I believe that this chamber is laid out exactly as the one on Level One,' observed Pryderi, as he examined the room. 'In that case this tunnel would be the Forbidden Zone of Level Seven. Do you know whether Level Seven had a Forbidden Zone, Stigand?'

The old man shook his head.

'I dwelt on Level Four before I was taken to Level One. And I have worked on Level Three. On those levels there were always Forbidden Zones. So perhaps Level Seven also has one.'

'Were the ones you knew of always in the same place?'

'Yes, I think so.'

Pryderi smiled. 'I believe, then, we have our means of escape. All we have to do is find Yaghus and Kigva.'

'You still don't know if Kigva is on Level Seven or, indeed, whether she has been captured by the Cynn at all,' Stigand pointed out. 'So your "all" is rather a lot. In these clothes we shall be spotted as escaped slaves within moments. How can we walk freely in Level Seven in order to find Yaghus or your sister?'

'Patience, Stigand. Perhaps we can steal some See-ti clothes.' It was Onnen who suggested this.

'That may be difficult,' said Stigand.

'Well,' Cador interrupted, 'we won't find out whether it is difficult or easy by standing here.'

Pryderi marched across the chamber pausing to examine the entrances of the two tunnels.

'This is the one, I think. I am trying to retrace the route which led to the chamber on Level One. I think the basic construction is the same on all levels.'

Without waiting for a reply, he set off down the tunnel, the girl and Cador following and with Stigand apprehensively bringing up the rear. Soon the tunnel began to lead downwards in a series of spirals and, as it did so, the air began to freshen. The passage was still thick with dirt and dust and their feet stirred whole clouds which now and then set them to coughing or sneezing. Finally the tunnel gave way to a straight passage that ended abruptly at a metal door.

Pryderi tried the handle but it refused to budge.

'We cannot get out,' observed Stigand with a moan. 'What can we do?'

'Your knife, Cador,' said Pryderi, ignoring the old man. Cador handed over his knife without a word.

Pryderi bent to the handle but found there was no lock. It was a door totally unlike anything he had seen in Lan-Kern. He examined all round for hinges but there were none. The door had an old, rusty quality to it and it came into Pryderi's head that the simple solution was brute force.

He stepped back a little and raised his foot, giving a sudden jabbing kick at the door. He felt it give slightly. He kicked again and again and on the fourth kick there was a scraping of ancient metal and the door pushed open a little way. Cador joined him as he put his shoulder to it and soon they managed to push it open wide enough for them to squeeze through one at a time.

The passage on the far side was less dirty and widened out into a broad way at the end of which a gleam of light could be seen. Pryderi switched off his torch and handed it to Stigand. They moved cautiously forward, keeping well to the sides of the tunnel as it opened wider.

At its mouth even Stigand exclaimed in astonishment at the vista that opened up. The tunnel emerged on a slight shelf some fifty feet above the ground level of the biggest cavern any of them had ever seen. Indeed, it was almost impossible to believe it was a cavern for it seemed that blue sky stretched overhead with billowing white clouds. Stigand pointed out that this was a filmed illusion which most levels occupied by the Cynn contained. As it was, however, they could hardly make out the far side of the cavern and only the most detailed examination of their surroundings revealed them to be in an enclosure at all.

'It is far, far bigger than the level on which I lived,' gasped Stigand.

Buildings of every sort and description, short and tall, stretched away into the distance. They were all built in some white stone. They could see people moving here and there. The start of this amazing complex of buildings was at least 150 yards from the cavern walls and in the intervening space was a park-like area, amazingly full of grass, shrubs and trees.

Pryderi roused them to a sense of immediate awareness.

'At least those will provide us with some cover. Let's get down and plan our next move.'

Cautiously, in semi-crouching positions they emerged onto the shelf of rock, overlooking the cavern, and found that one end of the shelf dipped sharply and merged into a series of smoothly cut steps. This stairway ran down to ground level. At the bottom of the steps was a board on which was painted a black skull and across the bottom the word '*Forbéodan*.' Breathlessly, they reached a clump of bushes in the park area and flung themselves down.

'Why,' cried Onnen, running her hand over the grass and then peering at the bushes, 'these are not real at all!'

'It would be amazing if real vegetation grew so deep beneath the earth,' pointed out Pryderi.

'What do we do now?' demanded Stigand.

'*Úp hand!*'

The voice was guttural. It belonged to a black uniformed guard who was standing not more than two yards away and covering them with the muzzle of his weapon.

It was lucky that Dryden chose to remain where he was after Thaec and Green hurried from the room. A few seconds passed before Thaec returned and Green with him.

'We'll recapture him, never fear,' Green was saying in English.

'He must be recaptured unharmed,' said Thaec angrily. 'He must still carry out the plan.'

'But how?' demanded Green. 'How will you persuade the man to kill Aldgyth?'

Thaec chuckled.

'I told you that the girl Kigva will do that.'

'I don't understand it completely.'

'When you first told me about this man Dryden I thought that he, like you, might be a useful recruit to the Cynn. After all, we need people who have knowledge of the surface in our armies. But the *Aelmihtig* showed me a different course. We captured a girl some time ago, a girl from Lan-Kern who is exceedingly pretty. As you know, Aldgyth has certain weaknesses ...'

Behind the drape Dryden chewed his lips in anguish. Kigva!

'It is merely another reason why Aldgyth must be removed. He pollutes the Cynn by relationships with inferior outlander women!' Thaec's voice was a snarl. 'It is immoral and disgusting!'

'Well?' prompted Green, for Thaec seemed to sink into silence as he contemplated the enormity of Aldgyth's crime.

'The girl was handed over to Aldgyth's household. By chance, as Dryden was returning from a questioning session with me, he saw the girl in Aldgyth's apartments. He told me that the very purpose he had come so far from Lan-Kern was his pursuit of this girl. It is evident that he is in love with her. I think it was then that my plan was born.'

'Yes,' sighed Green, impatiently. 'But I still do not see how it will work out exactly. You have only told me the general basis, which relies solely on the depth of Dryden's feelings for the girl.'

'I told Dryden that I would discover why the girl was in Aldgyth's apartments. I was letting him remain in apprehension for a while. Then I was going to tell him that Aldgyth had taken the girl as a plaything for a time. Think of the rage and frustration that would have built up in the man. Then, having brought him to a peak, I would have confided, in an unguarded moment, that no guards are allowed within the Faeder's apartment, and how easy it would be....' He gave a bark of laughter. 'I would have left him unguarded, left a weapon handy and placed my faith in the man's ingenuity. He would have found Aldgyth's apartments. I would have timed his escape so that he would reach there about the time Aldgyth retired for the rest period. He would have broken in and then - then our beloved Faeder would have been dead at the hand of a jealous lover, but - more importantly - by an outlander.'

Green shook his head.

'There are too many "ifs" arising from such a plan,' he said. 'Anyway, Dryden has escaped.'

'And my guess is he will try to get to Aldgyth's apartments. But the time is not opportune. He must be brought back. You wait here, Gréne. I shall go and organise a guard to prevent him gaining access to Aldgyth before we are ready.'

As Thaec left the room Green settled himself into a chair. For a moment or two Dryden did not move. His mind was filled with the enormity of the plot that Thaec had revealed. He quivered with frustration and anger as well as fear for the well-being of Kigva. Kigva! Weaponless as he was, he moved forward into the room.

Green heard the movement behind him, turned and then leaped from his chair.

'Dryden!' he gasped, his face paling.

Dryden's eyes narrowed as he stared at the former naval lieutenant.

'So you shot Harris?' he said coldly.

Green grimaced.

'It was his life or mine,' he defended himself. 'The young fool refused to accept the offer the Cynn made us. We could join them as equals or accept slavery and death. What would you have done?'

'The same as I have done already,' replied Dryden. 'The same as any moral man should do.'

'Morality? Rubbish! We are no longer in the twentieth century

- we are in a brutal new world, Dryden. Wake up to it. There's no moral code here. Life is cheap and the only code is survival.'

Dryden clenched and unclenched his hands.

'You're right, Green,' he replied. 'There is no moral code here. The Cynn are a cancerous, evil growth which must be eliminated before they destroy the good that remains in the world.'

'Still on the white charger, Dryden?' sneered Green. 'Still trying to right the wrongs of the world? That's a somewhat naive attitude. There is no right nor wrong, only that which is expedient.'

Dryden caught the flicker in the man's eyes as he observed Dryden was unarmed, a brief warning before Green's hand sped towards his weapon.

Dryden launched himself across the room, both hands flying to Green's wrist as he tried to level the pistol. Desperately, Dryden clung to Green's hand and both men crashed backwards over the chair in which Green had been sitting. For some moments they struggled and rolled across the floor as Dryden tried to twist the gun out of Green's hands. Then there came a muffled explosion and Green's body went suddenly limp.

Dryden lay still for fully a minute and then rose slowly to his knees, placing his fingers against the side of Green's neck. The man had no pulse. Dryden felt no emotion. He had lived among the *drewyth* of Lan-Kern too long to feel any satisfaction at the death of a fellow human being no matter how dastardly their crime. On the other hand, he felt no regret.

He picked up the pistol from Green's lifeless hand and examined it. It seemed to work on the basis of a twentieth century pistol but with small refinements. He recalled that Stigand had said that the Cynn had made little scientific progress since the Great Destruction and were merely utilising the weapons and machines of their ancestors without fully understanding how they worked nor how to replace them. He tucked the weapon in his belt.

It was a pity he had not been able to wrest any information from Green. He would have liked to know exactly where Aldgyth's apartments were. He would have to find them and rescue Kigva without being recaptured by Thaec's *weardian* or falling into the *thegn's* assassination plot.

He straightened himself and dusted away the marks of the combat

117

realising as he did so that he was dressed in the clothes of a Cynn. Outwardly there was nothing to tell that he was not of their number. Only if he were questioned would his speech betray him. Therefore he could merely go out into the passages and mingle with the other Cynn, there was no cause for anyone to stop him.

He bent down and gripped Green's arms, dragging the body into the alcove behind the drapes where he had hidden. That might buy him some precious time. He went to the door cautiously and it slid open for him. No one was standing outside in the brightly lit passageway. Squaring his shoulders he turned down the corridor and began to walk swiftly along it.

CHAPTER EIGHT

It was Cador who recovered the power of movement first. He was nearest to the *weardian* who now menaced them with his gun. The former war-lord of Lan-Howlek's figure became a sudden blur of motion as he ducked and rolled. It was the guard's turn to freeze in surprise for the *weardian* had not been trained to deal with outlanders who did not obey instructions. The *weardian* was still standing open-mouthed when Cador cannoned into him and landed a savage upper-cut to his jaw. The man collapsed to the ground without a word.

Pryderi hastened to the side of the fallen man and then glanced awkwardly at the grandson of Nelferch.

'Thanks,' he said shortly.

Cador shrugged and Pryderi turned back to the unconscious guard.

'Let's bind him to prevent him from doing further harm,' he suggested.

'What about his weapon?' asked Onnen.

Pryderi picked up the stick shaped object and looked at it with a puzzled frown.

'It shoots lightning bolts, apparently,' he mused. 'I have never seen the like of it before.'

'Cador and I have seen it in action,' said the girl.

'We call it a *gonne*,' interposed Stigand, as he watched them bind the guard and drag him behind some bushes for concealment.

'Do you know how to use it?' asked Pryderi.

'Not really,' confessed Stigand. 'I was never a *weardian*. I was a Level Four worker, an academic.'

Pryderi tossed the weapon in the bushes.

'Then let it stay there. We have no use for it.'

Onnen was looking around the park-like area in which they stood.

119

'What now?'

Having led the way to Level Seven in safety Pryderi was at a loss to know how to proceed. He turned to Stigand.

'How many people dwell on this level?'

Stigand pursed his lips.

'Only the élite of the Cynn - perhaps some ten thousand, that is all.'

Pryderi stared at him aghast.

'Ten thousand? Why, that is almost the entire population of Lan-Kern.'

Cador swore softly.

'It will be an impossible task to find two people here.'

Stigand nodded morosely.

'That is what I have said all along.'

'Is there any one building to which Yaghus would have been taken - a prison, the home of the *thegn*, for example?'

Onnen smiled. 'Yes, that is it. The girl Kigva and the man Yaghus might be held there. It is there that we should begin to look.'

Stigand did not look certain.

'You have some other idea?' pressed Onnen, looking at the old man.

'No; but how can we walk through the level?'

He paused and suddenly his eyes glistened.

'I have an idea. Underneath every level runs a series of sewers, underground tunnels. They cover the whole level. It is possible to traverse the entire level from one spot to another. We could journey to the *thegn's* apartments that way.'

'Well done, Stigand,' approved Pryderi. 'You feel able to find your way to the *thegn's* apartments through these sewers?'

'There is a certain point in the sewers where there is a map of the level which lists all the important places, for the assistance of the maintenance crews. We must find that first.'

'Good.'

Pryderi hesitated.

'Couldn't Yaghus have attempted an escape on Level One or Three by this means? Why didn't you mention these sewers before?'

'The sewers,' replied Stigand, slightly offended, 'only run on the living levels, that is Levels Seven, Six, Five and Four.'

120

Pryderi smiled and clapped the old man's shoulder.

'Well, you have given us a fine idea. Now here is another one.'

They looked at him expectantly.

'Stigand must don the uniform of the *weardian*. He is of the Cynn. If we encounter anyone he must pretend to be a guard taking us to the *thegn*.'

Onnen smiled her approval.

Stigand unwillingly changed his clothes for those of the still unconscious *weardian*. Then, with Stigand walking slightly behind them pretending to be their guard, they walked to the edge of the complex of buildings. They did not encounter anyone. Stigand called upon them to halt and pointed to a large man-hole cover. It was the work of moments to raise it and slip down the iron ladder into the darkness of the sewers. Stigand drew the cover shut over their heads and switched on the powerful torch he still carried from the Forbidden Zone.

At the foot of the ladder, Stigand stood hesitating.

'Where to now, old man?' asked Cador.

'Yes, where will the plan of the level be?' chimed in Pryderi.

'Not far from here,' replied Stigand. 'But - but there is one thing I must warn you of before we go further.'

'What is that?' demanded Pryderi, observing the uneasiness in the old man's eyes.

'We must beware of the *molle*.'

'The what?' asked Onnen.

'The *molle*,' repeated Stigand. 'How do you call them in your language - *goth*, moles.'

'Moles?' Onnen tried to suppress a smile. 'But moles are harmless creatures.'

'Not these,' said Stigand. 'They say the *molle* live in the sewers of all the levels from Seven to Four. They are *útlawe* - outlaws, people of the Cynn who reject the discipline of the Faeder. There is no way of escape from the See-ti, no way of going to the surface. Therefore those who do not wish to live under the Faeder, or be taken to the slave levels, take to the sewers, living in the dark tunnels, sometimes emerging, attacking and looting and even killing. But always they return to their lairs.'

Pryderi looked astonished.

'But surely the Cynn, the *weardian*, would be able to clear out the sewers?'

'It has been tried,' admitted Stigand. 'But no matter how many of the *molle* are caught others take their place.'

'So the *molle* are a resistance group to the Faeder and his supporters?' asked Pryderi.

'No,' Stigand shook his head vehemently. 'They are totally anarchistic. They have become mere animals, robbing, looting, murdering, as they fancy. Do you recall I mentioned my wife and daughter? When I was arrested I never saw them again. Well, I heard from another prisoner that they had fled to join the *molle*. *Aelmihtig!*'

He gave a sob.

Onnen took the old man's arm and pressed it in silent sympathy.

'We will have a care for the *molle*,' said Pryderi quietly. 'But our task is to find Yaghus and Kigva.'

Stigand drew himself together and nodded.

'Forgive me,' he whispered. 'I just meant to warn you. The plans should be this way.'

He led the way down a series of tunnels and then, abruptly, they found themselves in a large, dry vault, with several banks of instruments, dials and gauges in it.

'This should be the central control point for the sewers,' whispered Stigand as he stared about him.

Almost at once Cador pointed to a large rectangular board on which various designs were drawn. Stigand examined it eagerly.

'Yes,' he grinned excitedly. 'This is it. This is the plan of the sewers and each of the main buildings on this level is clearly marked. Here,' he jabbed with his finger, are the *thegn's* apartments and here is the building where the Faeder himself lives.'

Pryderi rubbed the back of his neck with his hand.

'It would save time,' he said reflectively, 'if we split up. Cador and Onnen could go to the *thegn's* apartments while Stigand and I could make sure that Yaghus has not been taken to the Faeder's place.'

'I have no objection,' agreed Cador, with a glance at Onnen, who nodded slightly.

'Right,' said Pryderi, 'make sure that you get your bearings clear from the plan. We will meet back here.'

122

Dryden forced himself to walk at a casual pace along the brilliantly illuminated corridors. He kept his eyes fixed firmly ahead and if anyone glanced at him suspiciously he muttered a *Gód daeg* in greeting and pressed on. He had traversed three long corridors before he came to a wide thoroughfare which looked vaguely familiar. His heart gave a bound as he realised that it was the very thoroughfare for which he was looking - the one in which he had seen Kigva at a window. He walked rapidly forward now, straight along the wide walkway, eyes darting here and there although he held his head still.

His pulse quickened when he saw the front of the building with the two lounging *weardian* outside. He forced himself to walk by it without faltering in his step and the *weardian* took no notice of him.

A few yards along the thoroughfare he turned into a small alley and halted, leaning against the wall and breathing rapidly. How was he to get into the Faeder's apartment building, surrounded as it was by guards? Get into it, he must. Kigva was there. The thought drove all else from his mind.

'*Illr sind éow, fréond?*'

Dryden turned and faced a pale man who was regarding him with some concern. He guessed, from the sound of the words, that the man was asking him whether he felt ill. Dryden pushed away from the wall and forced a smile.

'*Ná*,' he answered curtly in the Cynn negative, hoping it sounded natural. He turned and walked down the alley. At a corner he risked a glance over his shoulder and saw the man standing looking after him.

He turned the corner and, once out of sight, he halted and waited a moment. Then, peering back round the corner and seeing the man gone, he went back into the alley. He was sweating freely now. He walked up the alley towards the main thoroughfare. He had to get off the streets before someone discovered that he was an outlander. Perhaps the Cynn was even now telling the nearest *weardian* of his suspicions. But how was he to get into the Faeder's house? How was he to get past the guards? There seemed no way.

He saw a manhole cover in the alleyway and a thought suddenly came to him. The See-ti seemed to have a sewage system and perhaps they might also have a chain of connecting tunnels like any city of his own day and age. Perhaps those tunnels led under the house of the Faeder? He had a good sense of direction and he mentally measured the position of the manhole cover in relation to the main thoroughfare and then to the Faeder's house.

He turned back to the alley and bent over the black metal covering. There was an iron ring nestling in a slight depression. He glanced swiftly round, took the handle in a firm grip, pulled open the cover and climbed inside. There was a small iron ladder leading to the bottom of the shaft and once down a few steps he drew the cover down over his head.

The sewer was dark and smelled vile. He could see nothing and he closed his eyes for a moment, hoping to make them adjust to the darkness. When he opened them, to his surprise, he found he was able to see tolerably well in the gloom. Some soft light, a sort of phosphorus, seemed to glow from the walls of the dark, rounded passageway. Along the middle of it crept a stream of bittersweet, dank black water.

He climbed down the ladder to the passageway and tried to adjust his position to the alleyway above. A short distance along the tunnel, which apparently followed the route of the alleyway, opened into a wider tunnel running at right angles to it. Dryden mentally thanked the Cynn for their orderly planning: the tunnel obviously ran under the main thoroughfare. All Dryden had to do was estimate the distance of the Faeder's house along its hollow, echoing vaults.

Again he thanked the builders of the See-ti for, at measured points along the great tunnel, were smaller tunnels leading off. These went back only a matter of a few yards or so before ascending by means of steps. The stairways must obviously lead to the basements of the houses which lined the thoroughfare - if the houses had basements. He assessed that the third stairway along must be the one which led to the Faeder's apartments. He edged his way along the tunnel, trying to avoid the sewage, towards the stairway. It ended rather abruptly at a small metal door. Dryden saw that it was made of rusting iron. He felt over it and discovered a handle.

Cautiously, he tried it.

The handle would not move. He tried it again, exerting more pressure. There was a grating sound and the handle gave. Dryden breathed a sigh of relief and pushed. It gave only slightly, protesting with a terrifying screeching sound. Dryden threw his entire weight against the door and gradually it opened wide enough for his body to squeeze through.

The room he entered was darker than the sewer. He could dimly see rows of bottles. A wine cellar? No, for what would the Cynn know of wine? Nevertheless, he smelled alcohol. Beer? Yes, they could probably make a beer from yeast. He pushed through the room, wondering if he was indeed in the Faeder's apartments.

To his relief the door to the cellar opened easily and Dryden found himself in a dimly-lit storage area. Another door opened into a deserted kitchen. Dryden moved with extreme caution now, eyes and ears alert for any unexpected danger. A passage outside the kitchen door led to an ascending stairway at one end and a door at the other. He was about to pass into this passage when a harsh voice halted him. He slunk back into the kitchen and drew the door to.

A man was shouting in the guttural language of the Cynn. Another voice was answering respectfully. Dryden chanced a swift glance out into the corridor. Aldgyth himself was coming along the corridor with another man in the uniform of a *weardian*. Dryden drew back, heart beating rapidly. There was no time to hide if they entered the kitchen and indeed, nowhere to hide.

The Faeder and the *weardian* walked down the corridor past the kitchen door to the door at the further end. They paused a moment and then the *weardian* said: '*Gód daeg, mín Faeder.*' Then the door closed. Footsteps retraced their way back along the corridor and ascended the stairs.

Dryden waited a long time before he relaxed and drew a long breath. Silently, the Cynn weapon now in his hand, he moved out of the kitchen and crept down the corridor to the foot of the stairs. Aldgyth must have ascended these. Dryden climbed them carefully and found himself in a corridor from which several doors led to other rooms. Dryden paused, slightly confused. He had come from the cellar and now he supposed himself to be on the first floor of the building. He had seen Kigva at a second floor window. He turned to the next flight of stairs and ascended, wondering whether Aldgyth had continued upwards or whether he had gone into a room on the first floor.

One thing in his favour was the fact that there were apparently no guards within the building. He recalled Thaec having said as much and smiled grimly. Well, that was to his advantage now. He wondered briefly whether Thaec had discovered the body of Green and what the devious *thegn* of Level Seven was doing now. Dryden reached the head of the stairs and paused to listen. He could hear no sound. He took a few faltering steps down the corridor for, as on the first floor, he was faced with a series of doors leading off the corridor. He had just made a decision and moved to the nearest door, his hand already resting on the handle, when a scream momentarily froze him. It was a female scream and it came from further along the corridor.

He turned and raced to the door from behind which he judged the scream had come. Pausing for a moment to gather strength, he burst into the room.

Aldgyth turned round, a curse on his lips at the intrusion. Behind him, cowering before the Faeder of the Cynn and clutching her torn dress, her eyes wide with fear and an angry red weal on the pale skin of her cheek, was Kigva.

CHAPTER NINE

'Yaghus!'

Kigva's eyes lit with joy and relief.

Dryden's eyes flickered from Aldgyth to the girl. The Faeder, seeing Dryden's momentary distraction, started forward only to be halted by Dryden bringing up the firearm and jabbing it in his stomach.

'*Útlander docga*!' snarled the Faeder, then lapsing into halting *Kernewek*: 'You will pay for this intrusion!'

'I think not,' replied Dryden evenly. 'Are you all right, Kigva?'

'I will be all right now, Yaghus,' smiled the girl. 'Since I saw you this morning I have prayed to Bel that you would come for me. I have been in this awful Otherworld place for I don't know how long. I had given myself up for lost. Oh, but it is good to see you again, Yaghus.'

Aldgyth sneered.

'How touching. Look well upon each other for you will soon be dead.'

'Silence!' snapped Dryden, jabbing at the outraged Faeder with the muzzle of his gun. 'Has any hurt been done you by this man, Kigva?'

Kigva shook her head.

'Only just now - when he tried to -' She paused and shrugged.

Dryden leant forward until his face was within inches of the face of the Faeder of the Cynn. Then, without warning, he brought up his weapon and sent it crashing down onto the head of the startled man. Aldgyth grunted and dropped like a heavy sack to the floor. Dryden grabbed some drapes, tearing them from their hangings, and began to use them - cumbersome as they were - to bind the man's prostrate form.

'That will take care of him for a short while,' Dryden said grimly as he turned to the girl. 'The only way out of here is through the sewers, I'm afraid.'

'Sewers?' Kigva was puzzled and Dryden realised that such things did not exist in Lan-Kern. He briefly explained their purpose and Kigva's nose wrinkled in disgust but she squared her shoulders and indicated her readiness to follow him. He reached forward and took her hand.

'It is truly good to see you again, Yaghus,' she smiled. 'I never thought it possible. Life has become a nightmare since that day I was captured by the raiders from Lan-Howlek.'

'Nelferch was overthrown and my friend Cunobel now rules in Lan-Howlek while your father, Kesmur, is accepted as High Chieftain of all the tribes ...'

'And Cador?' breathed the girl.

Dryden shrugged.

'He escaped from Dynas Drok and was in pursuit of you. I do not know what has become of him. There is much to tell you, Kigva, but first we must leave here.'

'Lead and I will follow,' declared the girl.

Dryden gave her an encouraging smile and led the way back down the stairs to the lower levels of the house, into the kitchen and through to the cellars. Once at the entrance to the sewers he helped the girl past the rusting iron door and then turned to heave the door shut behind them.

'With any luck,' he declared, 'they will be unable to find out which way we have escaped.'

Kigva was looking around the sewer with obvious distaste.

'Which way do we go, Yaghus?'

Dryden did not want to let the girl know that he had absolutely no idea; no idea how he was even to get out of Level Seven let alone the See-ti. No idea how to get to Pryderi on Level One. He pointed at random: 'This way.'

They set off walking slowly along the eerie phosphorescence-lit tunnel. 'Great Bel the Lifegiver!' shuddered the girl as the foul air overwhelmed her. 'This is a vile place Yaghus.'

'How did they capture you?' asked Dryden, seeking to get the girl's mind away from the immediate problem.

She related the events of her escape from Dynas Drok and her capture by the Cynn.

'They brought me to this place and I was questioned by someone of high rank, a *thegn* I think they called him.'

'A tall, handsome man with bronze coloured hair?' queried Dryden.

'Yes, that is the man.'

'Thaec! He is more evil than Aldgyth!'

'That is difficult to believe,' replied Kigva. 'While I was being questioned by this *thegn*, Aldgyth entered. He is, apparently, the high chieftain here.'

Dryden did not bother to correct the girl's interpretation of the Faeder's role.

'Well,' continued the girl, 'Aldgyth demanded that I be given to him as a bond-slave. He merely lusted for me as a woman. Thanks be to Bel that, during the last few days - I am no longer certain how long I have been in this evil place - his duties kept him from pursuing his interest in me. Bel knows, Yaghus, what thoughts have been going through my mind. I thought of killing myself rather than submit to him. But,' she shrugged, 'what is the use of that? A crime against life is as great a crime as the one he intended. I tried to escape but I had no means. Then, can you imagine my feelings when, this morning, I saw you walking by the building? My hopes soared. I knew you would find a way of rescuing me. Then Aldgyth came. He dismissed his servants and staff and came to my room. I knew I was lost and made the futile gesture of screaming - suddenly you burst into the room.'

Dryden squeezed her arm.

'I thank Bel I arrived at that time, Kigva.'

'I, too, Yaghus.'

Then she lightened her voice.

'But, tell me, what happened at Dynas Drok? You say that Nelferch has been overthrown? I heard the start of the slave uprising before I fled from the fortress but I did not think they had any chance against Cador and his warriors. I thought you had been executed - that you had met your death at the hands of the *gourgath* as your reward for trying to rescue me.'

Dryden related how he had escaped and how he and the slaves

had risen against the old witch queen of Lan-Howlek. He went on to tell how Pryderi and he had left Lan-Howlek in search of Kigva and *An Kevryn* and how they had become captives of the Cynn. Kigva was pale.

'So Pryderi is now a slave in this place?' she asked slowly when Dryden had finished.

'Yes, on the first level, and I must devise a way of rescuing him.'

'It seems impossible,' the girl said morosely.

'Impossible?' Dryden made an attempt at a self-confident chuckle. 'It was thought impossible to rescue you, until it was accomplished.'

'But, Yaghus ...'

Dryden suddenly halted, his eyes searching the gloom ahead.

'What is it?' whispered the girl, seeing the look on his face.

'I thought I saw a movement - a human figure in the tunnel ahead of us.'

'But *mín thegn*,' pleaded the *weardian* who stood guard outside the door of the Faeder's residence, 'the Faeder left instructions that he was not to be disturbed on any account.'

'The authority is mine,' snapped Thaec. 'An outlander prisoner has escaped. He is known to have declared his intention of assassinating the Faeder.'

'But *mín thegn* ...' said the guard, unhappily, looking to his companion for support.

'Open the door, *weardian*, or suffer the consequences,' cried Thaec.

Reluctantly the guard stood aside and Thaec moved forward to open the door.

'Wait here, Wulfnoth,' Thaec snapped to his aide. Then, drawing his weapon, he hurried into the apartments of Aldgyth. He looked around him cautiously, wondering if the outlander had been there before him. Thaec was a good judge of character and he knew that Dryden possessed a certain stubborn streak which would put the odds of success in the outlander's favour. How else had he escaped and managed to kill Gréne? Well, Gréne was no great loss. He had been merely an efficient butcher and there were plenty of those. But Thaec's guards had searched the obvious places on Level Seven and the man had not been found. There was only one other obvious place that the outlander would have made for - the residence of Aldgyth.

It took Thaec some time, glancing into each room, before he opened the door of the upstairs chamber and saw Aldgyth lying in the torn drapes, struggling to escape from his bonds. Thaec let a slow smile spread across his handsome features as he stepped inside the room and drew the door to. So he had not overestimated the outlander! Aldgyth had managed to work loose his gag but, as the rooms of the Faeder were all soundproofed, it had not been to his advantage.

'Thaec!' gasped the man in relief, 'release me this instant - quickly man! It was the outlander - the one for whom you appear to display a fondness. He has escaped with the girl!'

'*Swá*?' breathed Thaec with satisfaction. Dryden had pulled off his rescue but that would not serve him for long. He would never be able to escape from the See-ti. But at least he had served Thaec's purpose. Everything fitted into his plan now.

'Thaec!' snapped the red-faced man on the floor. 'Untie me! Hurry!'

Thaec ignored the Faeder and walked over to a table, picking up a heavy metal statuette.

'What are you doing, Thaec?' A fear crept into the eyes of Aldgyth.

The *thegn* smiled slowly.

'What am I doing? Why, I am making myself the next Faeder of the Cynn.'

Aldgyth turned pale.

'What - what do you mean?'

'It is very simple, Aldgyth,' replied Thaec. 'The Cynn are about to return to the surface, to set out on the conquest of the world, to reclaim what is theirs by right. To do that, Aldgyth, they need a strong man; a man of iron will and purpose, one who will lead them well. They need a man whose will is absolute. I am that man, Aldgyth. You are merely a corrupt weakling who indulges in sensual pleasures with inferior beings. You contaminate the blood of the Cynn with your countless bastards. How can anyone as vile as you rule the world? It was destiny that the outlander broke in here and killed you.'

'But...'

Thaec raised the heavy statuette above his head and brought it down several times. Then he let it fall on the blood-splattered corpse of the former Faeder of the Cynn. For a moment Thaec gazed down at the body with a grim smile of satisfaction. Then he turned and modelled his face into an expression of dismay, going to the window and flinging it wide.

'Help!' he cried loudly. '*Weardian* - to me! Your Faeder has been murdered by the outlander! Help!'

He turned to the door and stepped into the corridor. He could hear them running up the stairs and adopted a posture of anguish.

'In there!' he gasped as the guards reached him. 'The outlander has murdered our Faeder.'

Wulfnoth followed with several more guards.

'Swiftly, guards, search the level for the outlander and his woman. Go, quickly now! We must avenge Aldgyth!'

Thaec laid a hand on Wulfnoth's arm to restrain him and they watched the guards disappear down the stairs and into the streets. They could hear the news being shouted outside.

Wulfnoth grinned at Thaec.

'What orders, *mín* Faeder?'

Thaec shook his head in rebuke.

'Not yet. Summon a meeting of the Witenagemot. They must first endorse me. But, in the meantime, let it be spread around the levels that I have been made Faeder of the Cynn by popular acclaim on Level Seven. That will bring any who would oppose my endorsement into line.'

Wulfnoth nodded, turned and then hesitated. He looked back at Thaec.

'Did the outlander - did he -?' He motioned in the direction of the chamber where Aldgyth's body lay.

Thaec gazed levelly back into the man's eyes.

'Who else, Wulfnoth?' he said evenly. 'Who else?'

CHAPTER TEN

Dryden felt Kigva's grip tighten on his arm.

'Look, Yaghus!' she whispered. 'There *are* figures moving in the shadows.'

Dryden reached for the Cynn gun in his belt. As his hand closed over the butt a harsh voice called out an order. It was obvious what the voice was ordering him to do. He took his hand away from the weapon.

Through the semi-gloom Dryden saw at least a dozen shapes crowding forward. Each dark figure seemed to hold a weapon of sorts. As they came close he saw that they were dark, swarthy men of stocky build. One of them, it was difficult to discern his features, came close, peering into their faces. He spoke rapidly but Dryden shook his head.

'*Útlanders?*' asked the man, enunciating the word slowly and clearly. Dryden nodded his affirmation. Hands ran over his body, feeling expertly for weapons and confiscating the gun in his belt.

'Who are you?' the speaker suddenly asked in the language of Lan-Kern. 'Who are you? I speak some of this outlander tongue. Do you speak also?'

'Yes,' replied Dryden. 'I am, as you say, an outlander. My name is Yaghus.'

The man peered at the girl.

'You?'

'I am Kigva of Lan-Kern.'

'Ah, *swá*? Lan-Kern. An outlander country.'

He turned back to Dryden.

'What you do here - here in sewers?'

Dryden hesitated. Should he be honest? These people did not look as though they were part of the Cynn system. Could they be escaped slaves?

133

'We are trying to escape from the See-ti!'

The man placed his hands on his hips and roared with laughter. Then he turned and obviously repeated what Dryden had said to his companions. For some minutes laughter echoed strangely in the tunnels.

'There is no escape from the See-ti, outlander. Never. You were slaves of the Cynn?'

'Yes.'

'*Swá*? I am Ecbert leader of the *molle* of *Tún seofen*.'

Dryden was puzzled.

'*Molle*?'

'We are outlaws. We rule the sewers. Here not even the *weardian* can go in safety. This is our domain. I am ruler,' he tapped his chest impressively. 'We are *molle* of the See-ti. All must beware of us.'

'You are against the Cynn? Against the Faeder?' asked Kigva.

'We are for ourselves,' replied the man called Ecbert.

'We are against the Cynn. We are trying to escape from them,' pressed the girl. 'Can you help us?'

'Why should we help you?'

'Because we have a common enemy,' replied Dryden.

'Enemy?'

'Yes, the Cynn.'

Ecbert laughed and translated this remark to his companions who also seemed to think it amusing.

'Is the sheep the enemy of the wolf?' smiled Ecbert. 'Like wolves we prey upon the Cynn. We have no common cause with anyone. Can you reward us for our help?'

Kigva nodded eagerly.

'My father is ruler of Lan-Kern. When I return to him he will see you well rewarded.'

'Return?' There was a sneer in Ecbert's voice. 'No one goes beyond Level One. No one goes to the surface. You will never return. Enough talk. You will come with us to our camp.'

He turned and started down the tunnel. The group of men closed in behind Dryden and Kigva and gave them a none too gentle push to start them forward. For some time they traversed passageways and tunnels until they finally came upon a large vault-like room which was fairly dry, unlike the sewage tunnels. It was crowded with bales and boxes. A number of women sat before fires which Dryden immediately recognised as a type of electric fire though Kigva stared at them in astonishment. The women looked up as the men entered with their captives. Questions were shouted and answered by the men, obviously boasting of their foray.

Ecbert, now revealed in the light of the vault, was a swarthy man, dirty and ill clad. Heavily armed, he swaggered with a conscious air of his position, speaking rapidly to the women and then turning to a young girl and speaking sharply to her. She turned towards Dryden and Kigva and, as she did so, they saw that she was quite young. In fact, Dryden placed her age at not more than fifteen. She was pretty beneath the covering of grime and dirt which seemed to be a common feature of the *molle*. Her short hair was plastered with filth and it was difficult to discern exactly what colour it was. She was clad in colourless dirt-stained rags. Ecbert moved away and the girl came across to them.

'I am Elgiva,' she smiled nervously. 'Do you speak this language?'

Both Dryden and Kigva nodded as the girl spoke hesitantly in the *Kernewek*.

'Ecbert, our leader, says that I am to look after you.'

She pointed to a corner of the chamber.

'This way. You will be comfortable here.'

'Are we prisoners, Elgiva?' asked Dryden as they followed the young girl to the corner which she had indicated, away from the main group of *molle* who were now gorging themselves with food prepared by their women. They could also see that a great deal of drinking was in evidence.

'Prisoners?' The young girl sighed wistfully. 'We are all prisoners. Sit here. Are you hungry?'

Kigva nodded and the girl went off, returning shortly with bowls of steaming liquid. It was the inevitable yeast soup. The girl also brought with her hunks of heavy yeast-loaf.

'Who are these people, Elgiva?' asked Kigva, between mouthfuls of the food.

'The *molle*,' returned the girl. 'People who live outside the laws of the Cynn. They live in the sewers of the levels of the See-ti, robbing and murdering to stay alive. They - they are animals!'

The young girl shuddered violently.

'You are not a *molle* then?' asked Dryden, noticing that the girl had disassociated herself from the others. Tears formed in Elgiva's eyes.

'I am not of this level,' she whispered in reply.

Kigva had reached out to press the girl's arm, moved by the unhappiness in her face.

'Not of this level?' she asked.

'I was stolen from an upper level during a raid when Ecbert led his *molle* against the *molle* of my level. That was a year ago or more. That beast - Ecbert - slaughtered my mother and many of the *molle* of our level.'

'You were always a *molle*?' asked Dryden intrigued.

'As far as I remember,' replied the girl. 'But my mother told me that once we were a well respected Cynn family. But my father disagreed with the Cynn and they punished him by taking him to the slave levels. Before they came to arrest him, my father pressed my mother to escape lest she suffer a similar fate. There was only one way to escape - to flee into the cellars and sewers and join the *molle*. The *molle* are the only alternative to the Cynn. My mother told me that we became *molle* when I was about four or five. I cannot really remember anything before that time. I grew up in the sewers of my own level - until the day that Ecbert raided us.'

The girl lapsed into sobs and Kigva placed her arm around Elgiva's heaving shoulders.

But Dryden's mind was working at a rapid pace.

'Elgiva,' he pressed, ignoring the girl's sobs, 'how did Ecbert manage to get from this level to yours?'

The girl paused at the intensity of his voice and sniffed.

'Why, through the Forbidden Zone of course'.

'The Forbidden Zone?' Dryden felt a growing excitement. 'Elgiva, is it possible to go from one level to another, say all the way up to the first level of the See-ti, through this Forbidden Zone?'

The girl frowned.

'I don't know. The *molle* usually confine themselves to the lower levels where the Cynn dwell. There is no point in going to the slave levels. But I suppose it is possible.'

Dryden smiled broadly.

'And perhaps, through this Forbidden Zone, it might be possible to go to the surface?'

'I have never heard of such a thing,' replied the girl with a shake of her head.

Dryden sat back undismayed.

'I think we have our means of escape at last,' he whispered to Kigva.

Elgiva frowned at him, overhearing.

'Escape?'

Dryden nodded with a smile.

'Elgiva, would you like to escape from Ecbert?'

'I dream of little else,' the girl replied quietly.

'Could you lead us to the Forbidden Zone and show us how to go from one level to another?'

'Elgiva! *Cuman!*' Ecbert's harsh voice came from the far side of the chamber.

Elgiva glanced round guiltily.

'Soon they will all be asleep,' she whispered. 'The drink renders them like dead things. When they are asleep I shall lead you to the Forbidden Zone.'

She turned and made her way to where Ecbert lay sprawled with a woman. *'Béor!'* cried the leader of the *molle,* throwing a flagon at the girl. She caught it deftly and went to fill it from a large barrel nearby.

It seemed an age before a silence fell in the chamber - a silence punctuated by the drunken snores of the sleeping *molle* and their women.

After a half-hour of undisturbed snoring Elgiva rose to her feet and made her way to where Dryden and Kigva sat. She placed a finger to her lips and indicated the entrance.

'At least they did not think to bind us,' whispered Dryden, as he and Kigva followed the girl.

'They are stupid animals, these *molle*,' Elgiva said over her shoulder.

She led the way out into the dark tunnel but they had hardly gone more than a few yards when a cry made them halt. Their hearts sank.

'Stop, outlanders!'

Dryden turned to see the swaying figure of Ecbert standing

drunkenly in the archway through which they had just come. He was struggling to reach for a weapon in his belt.

Dryden did not hesitate. He leapt upon the man. The two of them fell to the bottom of the tunnel, into the stream of murky sewage. In spite of his drunkenness, Ecbert was a man of powerful strength and two iron hands seized Dryden about the throat, forcing his head back under the awful black water. Dryden struck up in desperation, trying to loosen the man's grip.

Kigva and Elgiva stared as the two men threshed about in the muck of the sewer tunnel. For a while Dryden's main thought was to prevent Ecbert from crying out a warning to his men. He clung on to the man with grim determination. Finally Ecbert's state of inebriation began to show. He sweated too freely, his breath came in gasps and his powerful fingers seemed to weaken their hold.

With one desperate lunge Dryden seized the man's head and thrust it into the water and managed to hold it there. After a while, Ecbert's body was still. Dryden heaved himself to his feet, trying to fight the awful well of sickness that swept through him. He eventually became aware of Elgiva tugging at his hand.

'This way, we must hurry before the others discover his body. Quickly, quickly now!'

Automatically, Dryden turned after the girl, Kigva gripping his arm, as Elgiva hurried along the dark tunnel, following its twisting route with swift certainty. Dryden lost all sense of time and distance. That some minutes elapsed he knew, for he and Kigva were beginning to tire. Several times Elgiva paused and stood listening.

Dryden asked: 'What is it?'

'I think I hear someone following,' whispered the girl in reply. 'You become attuned to noises and their identities when you live down here.'

Dryden screwed his eyes into the blackness behind them.

'The *molle*?'

'I think not. They do not travel with caution. Perhaps the *weardian*.'

'Let's go on,' urged Kigva.

They hurried on and were rounding a corner of the tunnel when the light of a torch suddenly beamed on them, causing them to halt and blink in confusion.

138

Trying to shade his eyes with his hand, Dryden could make out only two shadowy figures behind the light.

One of the figures gave a startled cry.

'The girl is Kigva - I *know* her!'

The torch was switched off and Dryden strained forward in the gloom to examine the two figures.

It was Kigva who recognised the speaker first.

'Bel protect us!' she gasped, taking an involuntary step backwards. 'Cador - Cador of Lan-Howlek!'

The former warlord of Lan-Howlek stepped forward, a frown creasing his dark face as he started towards Dryden. For a moment they formed a motionless tableau. Then, with a muffled exclamation, Cador of Lan-Howlek reached for the knife in his belt, drew it and threw it with full force at Dryden.

PART THREE

The Destruction

"One man builds. Another man tears down. A whole age can be destroyed within a minute. Creation and destruction; surely these go hand in hand for both are demonstrations of power. And yet of the two it is destruction that is the easiest way of demonstrating power and is held in awe by mankind. Armies forging empires destroy civilisations and are regarded with admiration and reverence through the ages for their obliterations. Thus man will ever destroy man."

An Lyver Mur a Lan-Kern
The Great Book of Lan-Kern.

CHAPTER ONE

Thaec gazed around the crowded chamber of the Witenagemot, the supreme ruling council of the Cynn, and shrugged modestly.

'I am not worthy to be Faeder,' he smiled, shaking his head.

At once a chorus of protests greeted him. They arose mainly from the section of *eorls* rather than Thaec's fellow *thegns*, who now glanced nervously at each other. Wulfnoth, who was the premier *eorl*, stood up.

'The Cynn already proclaim you their Faeder through the levels of the See-ti,' he called and others shouted agreement. 'There is no one better than you, Thaec, to lead our people to their predestined glory.'

'It is the will of the Cynn!' cried one of the *eorls*.

Thaec stood, hands on hips, and looked slowly round the chamber.

'If it is the will of the Witenagemot...?'

A tumultuous roar greeted him. Thaec turned to his six fellow *thegns*, his eyes questioning. One by one they nodded their assent.

'Then I accept the wisdom of your choice,' declared Thaec.

He held up his hands to quell the cheering of his supporters.

'My first task as your Faeder must be to seek out and destroy the outlander who has so cruelly robbed us of one of our greatest leaders. My *weardian* will scour all levels for the man called Dryden. The sewers as well will be flushed out - they will be purged of the evil canker they contain. The *molle* are an affront to the dignity of the Cynn!'

Wulfnoth was on his feet again.

'Even as you speak, *mín* Faeder, it is being done.'

'Good!' returned Thaec. 'And my second task is to mobilise the Cynn. Yes, the time has come to start our great mission to reclaim the world for our own as it was ordained by our great ancestors who preserved us, the élite of humankind, from the Age of the Great Destruction!'

One of the *thegns* rose half-heartedly to his feet.

It was Hasculf, *thegn* of Level Four.

'Thaec,' he began and then corrected himself. '*Mín* Faeder - surely we are not prepared to commence this task at this time. It was an argument of Aldgyth, the *Aelmihtig* give him peace, that we had not yet developed our full capability for this task?'

One or two *thegns* half nodded but dropped their eyes beneath Thaec's stern glance.

'Aldgyth was a great leader,' acknowledged Thaec, a cynical smile playing on his lips. 'But in this matter he was grossly misled by certain place-seekers. Those men,' Thaec looked a long time at the *thegns*, 'those men I have noted. They have long delayed the hour when the Cynn should have struck. And I, who am now Faeder by the will of the people, say the time has come. We will strike now!'

There was a chorus of approval from the *eorls*.

'Within two rest periods,' declared Thaec, 'our battalions will commence to gather on the surface. When they have gathered, I shall lead them westward - I, personally, shall lead them to the conquest of the first outlander countries. We shall destroy Lan-Kern and Lan-Howlek!'

The entire chamber rose up in a thunderous applause as the handsome Cynn leader, now undisputed Faeder of his people, stood smiling in heroic pose before the Witenagemot.

Dryden heard Kigva scream and felt the rush of air as Cador's knife sped by his cheek.

Before he could react there was a cry behind him and he turned his head. To his astonishment, he saw the black shape of a *weardian* falling to the ground, the knife buried in the man's chest, and a weapon falling from his nerveless grasp.

'Quickly!' cried Cador. 'There are more of them coming along the tunnel!'

Dryden could hear their cries and the stamp of their boots.

Dryden turned to Cador in amazement. Kigva was holding on to his arm tightly. There was fear in her eyes as she gazed at the figure of the former warlord of Lan-Howlek.

The second figure moved forward. It was a fair-haired girl.

'For the sake of Bel, come quickly!' she urged. 'Whatever Cador has done to you in the past, do not think of it now. He has no remembrance of it. Trust him as your friend until I can explain'.

Elgiva tugged at Dryden's arm.

'Oh quickly! They are nearly upon us!' she implored.

Dryden nodded.

'Very well. Lead on.'

He detached Kigva's arm from his and bent to recover the weapon dropped by the *weardian*.

'I will lead,' cried Elgiva, moving forward. 'I know how we may lose them.'

She moved away swiftly with the others following, turning and twisting through the tunnels until they came to a small cave-like room which lay beyond a narrow passage.

'We will be safe in here awhile,' gasped the young girl.

They pushed into the small room and collapsed in breathless heaps on the floor.

Kigva was still staring at Cador with loathing. Cador noticed Kigva's expression and flushed.

'I do not remember,' he muttered uneasily. 'Yet I recall your face. I recall you as Kigva and know that I had to find you.'

Kigva almost cringed before his gaze and he turned his head away from her in confusion.

'Have I hurt you that much?' he whispered, forcing the words.

'More than you could ever repay, Cador of Lan-Howlek,' returned the girl with venomous hatred.

Dryden turned to the fair-haired girl.

'You'd better explain. Do you know this man, Cador? Has he truly lost his memory?'

Onnen sighed and made an affirmative nod before she introduced herself and told them, as briefly as she could, everything that had happened since her meeting with Cador.

'You say that Pryderi is down here - in the sewers searching for us?' gasped Kigva as Onnen finished her narrative.

'Yes.'

'Can you find your way back to the control room?' asked Dryden.

'I can,' interposed Elgiva. 'I can find my way anywhere.'

145

'Then we'd better go in search of Pryderi and Stigand,' suggested Dryden.

Cador leaned forward. Throughout Onnen's narrative both Dryden and Kigva had studiously ignored him. Now he reached out a hand and laid it on Dryden's arm.

'I am sorry for what I have done in the past, Yaghus,' he said earnestly. 'Perhaps that sounds weak. I do not know for I do not know what I have done to you. Accept my assurance that I am with you now.'

Dryden caught Onnen's pleading look and shrugged.

'You cannot ask me to forgive and forget, Cador,' he said slowly. 'However, let there be a truce between us until we talk with Pryderi.'

He rose to his feet.

'Let us move as soon as possible.'

Elgiva placed a finger to her lips and went to the entrance, pausing to listen. All was silent.

'I think the *weardian* have gone now,' she said. 'Follow me carefully.'

They walked rapidly along several tunnels. For the first time in an age Dryden felt light-hearted. Kigva was by his side and escape from the See-ti was imminent. He turned to Onnen.

'You say that you came down from the surface directly to Level Seven?'

Onnen smiled.

'It was your friends, Pryderi and Stigand, who discovered the method. There was some sort of small room which moves upwards and downwards according to your will.'

'An elevator?'

'I think that is what Stigand called it.'

'Then we can escape to the surface?'

'Yes. I believe so.'

It seemed a long time before Elgiva halted and motioned them to be quiet.

'Around the corner is the control room,' she whispered.

Cador looked round eagerly.

'Yes, the girl is right. I recognise this tunnel now.'

Dryden moved cautiously forward and strained around the corner of the tunnel.

'There doesn't seem to be anyone there,' he reported.

They moved slowly into the vaulted chamber and stared around them.

'We will have to wait,' declared Cador. 'Pryderi and Stigand said that they would return here.'

Kigva bit her lip.

'What if they have been captured by the Cynn or the *molle*?' she asked. 'What if...'

There was a movement behind them.

As they whirled about a figure in the black uniform of a *weardian* entered. His gun was already levelled in his hands.

'Any news, Wulfnoth?' demanded Thaec, glancing up as his aide entered the empty chamber of the Witenagemot. Thaec sat morosely in the great chair used by the Faeder during the council sessions.

'No word yet, *min* Faeder,' replied the *eorl*. 'One of our patrols reports that one of their men has been murdered in the sewers.'

'The *molle*?' queried Thaec.

'He was stabbed with an outlander knife.'

'That doesn't mean anything. Anyway, where would Dryden have obtained such a weapon?'

Wulfnoth shook his head.

'Are the battalions mobilising?'

Wulfnoth grinned.

'They are, *mín* Faeder. At the end of the next rest period they will be ready to start transportation to the surface. Soon the entire Cynn will be on the march.'

Thaec banged his hands together.

'*Aelmihtig*!' he declared. 'Excellent! Soon Lan-Howlek will fall to us and then Lan-Kern. This day has been too long delayed, Wulfnoth. Aldgyth was a weakling. A foolish indolent man. He preferred the degenerate pleasures of the body to fulfilling his great mission.'

'It was not his destiny, *mín* Faeder,' grinned Wulfnoth. 'That destiny is yours. You will be acclaimed as the greatest of the Faeders of the Cynn.'

Thaec took a moment to preen himself in response to the *eorl's* flattery.

'After my meal, Wulfnoth,' he said, 'I will start an inspection of all levels, including the slave levels. I must ensure the readiness of our people.'

Wulfnoth saluted and withdrew, leaving Thaec to his meditation.

The *weardian* emerged into the chamber and peered in astonishment at the group gathered there.

Dryden was trying to reach for his weapon surreptitiously when the *weardian* held up a hand.

'It is I - Stigand!'

The old Cynn came forward, taking off his cap so that they could recognise him. A moment later Pryderi joined them and, for a while, the entire party became oblivious to their surroundings and to time, as they exchanged greetings, introductions and individual tales. It was only with some difficulty that Stigand managed to make himself heard.

'Listen, Yaghus,' he said, 'while I do not regret the passing of Aldgyth, I think that by killing him you have created greater problems.'

Dryden looked at Stigand thunderstruck.

'Me kill Aldgyth? But I did no such thing,' he protested.

Kigva moved forward.

'I was there. Yaghus did not kill him. We left him bound but alive.'

Stigand frowned.

'When Onnen and Cador left in search of you at *thegn* Thaec's apartments, Pryderi and I went to the Faeder's apartments. I managed to overhear some of the *weardian* talking. They said that the Faeder had been murdered by an outlander who had escaped with an outlander woman. They said that the *thegn* Thaec had discovered the body.'

Dryden snapped his fingers.

'Thaec! Of course, Thaec had planned that I should kill Aldgyth in order that he could assume the Faedership. I believe that as I didn't oblige him he killed Aldgyth himself and claimed that I had done it.'

Stigand scratched his nose.

'It could be so. Thaec has been made Faeder, so the *weardian* said. Moreover, he has ordered a full-scale search for you.'

'Then we had better make for this place called the Forbidden Zone,' said Dryden. 'We must escape as soon as possible to warn Kesmur and Cunobel of the plans of the Cynn to attack them.'

Stigand held out a hand to stay Dryden as he turned away.

'There will not be time for that, Yaghus,' he said heavily.

Dryden turned back with a questioning look.

'What do you mean, Stigand?'

'From the same guards, I overheard that Thaec, as Faeder, has ordered the full mobilisation of the Cynn. Even now the Cynn are preparing to mass for the attack on Lan-Kern.'

Pryderi turned an anguished face to Dryden.

'It is so, Yaghus. We will have no chance against the Cynn with their infernal Otherworld gadgets - their lightning bolts and their flying machines.'

There was a long silence.

It was finally broken by the young girl, Elgiva, not understanding the import of their words.

'Why do we not go to the Forbidden Zone?' she asked nervously. 'We will soon be discovered if we remain here.'

Kigva stirred.

'The girl is right. We must try to save ourselves. Perhaps we can think of a way to stop the Cynn later.'

Stigand heaved a deep sigh.

'Stop the Cynn? There is no stopping the Cynn. You outlanders do not have the technology, the advanced weaponry of the Cynn. You do not have the means of comprehending it. The Cynn are invincible.'

'Perhaps there is a way to stop the Cynn before they gather on the surface?' pressed Pryderi.

'Yes,' chimed in Cador. 'Maybe we could destroy those moving rooms which you call elevators?'

Stigand shook his head.

'Destroy the elevators? They are impregnable against such attacks. They were built by our ancestors to withstand the onslaught of ages. There is no way, no way at all, of stopping the Cynn.'

149

CHAPTER TWO

Dryden was surprised at the comparative ease with which they managed to make their way through the sewers, led by Elgiva, and out of the entrance bordering on the park area which fronted the entrance to the Forbidden Zone. Luck was with them all the way because they met no *weardian* patrols and there was no sign of any Cynn when they climbed from the manhole and ran into the shelter of the synthetic park. Behind the cover of the trees and shrubs they halted to regain their breath before tackling the short climb into the Forbidden Zone tunnel.

As they squatted in the bright lights of Level Seven, Stigand gazed upon the face of Elgiva and a curious expression began to change his features. It was the first time he had seen the face of the girl clearly. The young girl caught his scrutiny and frowned.

'What is it?' she demanded. 'Why do you stare so?'

Stigand scratched his temple.

'It is just - just that you remind me of someone I used to know so long ago.'

The girl gave a contemptuous shrug but then some distant memory stirred in her mind and she turned and gazed deeply into Stigand's eyes. Abruptly Stigand's eyes moistened, his lips trembled.

'How old are you, my child?'

'They tell me I am fourteen years of age,' replied the girl.

'And your mother? What was her name? What level were you born on?'

'My mother died last year,' said the girl. 'She was called Edburga of Level Four.'

An expression almost of pain crossed Stigand's face.

'Did Edburga - did your mother ever tell you about your father; tell you his name?'

To the astonishment of the others, who had been unable to follow this conversation, which had been in the language of the Cynn, Elgiva burst into a choked laugh, a cross between a laugh and a great sob, and flung herself into the old man's outstretched arms.

Stigand pressed her closely and mumbled through his tears: 'Thanks be to the *Aelmihtig*!'

The others sat in silence, not knowing the cause of the moving scene, as father and daughter found each other after ten years of separation. Finally, Stigand explained haltingly to Dryden. He hated to intrude upon the moment but time pressed.

'Once we are on the surface there will be plenty of time for a proper reunion,' he said gruffly.

Stigand smiled through his tears: 'She whom I thought was lost to me entirely is found, Yaghus. I will die content now.'

With Dryden's urging, they hurried past the *'Forbéodan'* sign, up the steps to the rock shelf, through the ancient metal door and into the tunnel. Here Pryderi took the lead and soon brought them into the chamber with its banks of dusty instruments and the lift shaft.

This time it was Dryden's turn to delay as he stared about the chamber in astonishment. The theories which he was forming about the origins of the See-ti were irrevocably confirmed. Most of the signs were in the English of his world. 'Emergency Exit'; 'Radiation Control'; 'Airlock Systems' and so forth were borne on various metal-plated inscriptions. 'Sterile Suits' was the legend under the rack of what reminded Dryden of space suits. He shook his head in amazement. So the See-ti had been built as an underground shelter complex in which the privileged had survived the age of the Great Destruction. But what was the Great Destruction? How had it come about?

'Come on, Yaghus,' urged Kigva, peering around with a shudder. 'Let us be on our way from this accursed place.'

'Yes,' agreed Pryderi. 'We must tell our people to prepare to meet the attacks of the Cynn as soon as we can.'

Dryden nodded absently, his eyes still wandering over the control banks. One metal cabinet was marked 'Emergency Explosives' and nearby 'Self-Destruct Level 7'. He turned and joined the others who were waiting impatiently in the elevator. His mind was a turmoil of thoughts as they sped upwards. The elevator shaft, the so-called

151

'Forbidden Zone', had obviously been constructed as an emergency exit from the great shelter complex which was now called the See-ti. It was incredible. Those people who, for whatever reason, had been selected to go down into the shelter - surviving the inevitable outcome of man's petty squabbling and playing with forces beyond his control - had evolved into the Cynn. How long had they been down in their shelter? A thousand years, two thousand - three thousand? Dryden shuddered. And all that time they had been evolving, evolving their strange philosophy, building a new culture, a new mythology and eventually finding a means to return to the surface in order to dominate the world.

It was late afternoon judging by the position of the sun in the sky. They emerged near to the camp where Pryderi and Stigand had encountered Onnen and Cador. Stigand felt a little dizzy in the daylight but was able to control his feelings thanks to the experiments he had taken part in to help the Cynn adjust their eyes to surface light again. With Elgiva it was different. Not only had the girl lived all her life in the See-ti but most of it had been spent in the darkened sewers. She cried out in pain as the light struck her eyes.

It was Onnen who wrapped a cloth around the girl's eyes and led her and Stigand to the shelter of some trees whose nearness made them feel better, although Stigand trembled a little at the emptiness of the vista. It would be difficult to adjust, observed Dryden. It was Stigand who found the solution to Elgiva's sensitivity to the light. He was still wearing his *weardian* uniform and, fumbling through its pouches, he found the eye shades which the guards used in their raids on the surface. Having put them on, Elgiva, perhaps because of her youth, proved more adaptable to the new conditions.

'It was found,' smiled Stigand, 'that if one stayed on the surface for fourteen surface days, wearing these shades, that one could adjust over that time to the surface light with the naked eye.'

'I'll get some water,' declared Onnen, turning towards a stream. 'We could all do with some refreshment.'

Water!

Dryden jerked his head up from the whirling thoughts within his mind.

Water! The self-destruct mechanism for each level! Flooding!

The plan presented itself in his mind without any evolution.

'I think you have just told me how we can stop the Cynn,' he said slowly.

They stared at him curiously.

'Do you agree that the Cynn must be stopped from their attempt to conquer the world? Do you agree that their technology, their weaponry is so advanced that it will be difficult to stop their conquest by an attempt to meet them in battle?'

'The answer is "yes" to both questions,' Pryderi said, acting as spokesman. 'But you already know this, Yaghus.'

'Very well. I know the means to destroy the Cynn and the See-ti.'

'A way to destroy the See-ti?' gasped Stigand. 'How is that possible? Our ancestors built the See-ti as an indestructible bulwark against the ravages of all times.'

Dryden smiled.

'Yet in their infinite wisdom, Stigand, they provided a way of destroying it. And you, yes you, Stigand, told me how.'

'I?' Stigand was astonished.

'From where does the See-ti get its water supply?'

'It is true that I did tell you that,' agreed Stigand. 'There is a great reservoir built underground which is fed by rivers and streams whose water is constantly filtered to make it drinkable. This storage area supplies other reservoirs built for each level, so that each level has a separate water supply. Even at each level the water undergoes a purification process which is a method known only to the ancients who devised it.'

'How would this aid in destroying the See-ti?' Onnen asked.

'Stigand will tell you how the water is controlled.'

Stigand raised his arms and then dropped them.

'As I pointed out to you before - the control panels by the main elevators have a section which houses the environmental and atmosphere controls. The operators there control the flow of water into the individual level and the flow of waste water out of the level.'

'We could destroy the controls and flood the levels,' declared Dryden.

'Flood the levels?' whispered Stigand. 'Drown the Cynn? But that is not possible!'

'Kill all those people?' Pryderi was horrified.

Cador laughed cynically.

153

'Rather they be drowned now than our people be destroyed in the future.'

'But such a thing is impossible,' asserted Stigand. 'The ancients who built the See-ti provided against all accidents. There are two safety valves to every level controlling the flow of the water. If you destroyed the control panels then the safety valves would be activated. It is a futile idea, Yaghus. Even if the safety valves were destroyed the water would not flow through them at any great rate.'

'I told you that your ancients provided a way of destroying the See-ti,' repeated Dryden. 'When we came through the Forbidden Zone I saw a self-destruct mechanism for each level. I saw it briefly but what it did say was that the self-destruct mechanism was somehow fitted to the water tanks which would flood the See-ti. Each level has an explosive device which has to be operated separately, flooding one level at a time.'

'Explosive?' the technological concept was beyond Pryderi. Only Stigand understood the meaning of explosives.

He shook his head.

'But those devices were built by the ancients thousands of years ago,' he protested. 'They would not work now.'

Dryden shrugged.

'I think your ancients built things to last, Stigand. Anyway, we must try. I believe it is our only chance to save the world from an eternity of bloodshed.'

Stigand scratched his forehead.

'It is hard for me to think about it, Yaghus. In other words you plan to destroy the entire See-ti - friend and foe alike.'

Dryden gazed at the worried faces turned towards him.

'Is there an alternative?' he asked. 'It is a hard decision to make but we must take into account the maxim of the greatest good for the greatest number. We know what will happen if Thaec and his Cynn start their wars of conquest. Lan-Howlek and Lan-Kern will be the first to fall beneath their yoke and who knows how long it will be before the Cynn will be overthrown or, indeed, whether they ever will be overthrown?'

'So some who are innocent must perish if the greater evil is to be avoided?' observed Kigva.

Dryden bit his lip. 'That is the decision to be made.'

'But I still cannot see how you can destroy the See-ti,' put in Cador.

'Leave that part of it to me,' replied Dryden. 'Our first task is to make the decision whether to destroy the Cynn now, resulting in the destruction of their entire world - good and bad, guilty and innocent. Or merely to flee west and hope that our people will be able to stand up against them in battle when the time comes.'

There was a silence while each examined their own consciences.

It was Stigand who stirred first.

'I am of the Cynn,' he said slowly, 'and therefore I have the right to speak first.'

Receiving no interruption he continued.

'It is as Yaghus says. The evil is too great, the threat too immediate. The Cynn must be destroyed if it is at all possible.'

He dropped his head and stared at the ground.

Dryden laid a hand on the old man's shoulder. Then he turned to look at Pryderi.

'This is against the teaching of Bel, against my belief as a *drewyth*,' the young man said. 'Nevertheless ...' He nodded. 'I say - destroy them,' said Cador vehemently. 'And I,' echoed Onnen. Kigva gave a wan smile to Dryden. 'The greater good for the greater number,' she said softly.

Dryden drew himself up.

'Very well. I shall attempt to carry out my plan.'

'One moment,' Stigand interrupted. 'I am a Cynn - and I have just condemned my people, all my people, to death. Let me, at least, try to save some of the innocent. Let me try to save some of those pitiful few who dwell on the slave levels.'

Dryden frowned.

'How can you do this without warning the Cynn of our intention?'

'I must try,' replied Stigand. 'You must see that, Yaghus? Let me try to coincide with the time you commence your attempt to destroy the See-ti. You recall the loudspeaker system on which orders to the slaves were broadcast?'

'Yes,' answered Dryden.

'If I could seize control of that and broadcast to the slaves of all three levels - I could tell them to flee to the elevators and make their way to the surface.'

155

'Where would you have to seize control of the speakers?'

'On Level Three.'

'Very well,' said Dryden. 'Cador and I will first try to activate the self-destruct mechanisms on the bottom four levels. Pryderi and Stigand will wait for us on Level Three and will attempt to take over the speaker system and warn the slaves. Then we carry out the destruct systems on the next three levels.'

'What will we do, Yaghus?' demanded Onnen. 'Is there nothing we can do to help?'

'Yes,' smiled Dryden. 'You, Kigva and Elgiva will remain here until it is over. If we fail in any way then you must do your utmost to get to Cunobel in Dynas Drok and warn him and also Kesmur of Lan-Kern. But I fear that if we fail in this task, the future will be a bloody one.'

He turned to his companions.

'Are you ready?'

They grunted their assent.

Onnen embraced Cador and Kigva kissed Pryderi on the cheek. There was a touching parting between Stigand and his new found daughter Elgiva. Dryden found himself dropping his eyes in embarrassment and turned to go.

'Yaghus!'

Kigva's whisper made him turn. The girl smiled at him, reached forward, raising herself on tiptoe, and let her soft lips brush his cheek.

'Come back safely.'

Dryden felt a warmth go through him.

'I'll be back,' he promised.

CHAPTER THREE

The short journey to Level Three was accomplished without mishap. At Level Three Dryden paused to examine the control systems to make a comparison with those on Level Seven. They were exactly the same. There, in clear English, was an ancient metal disc on which 'Shelter Self-Destruct Mechanism' was stamped. Underneath this inscription was a set of five instructions on how to operate the mechanism. Finally, following the instructions were the words: 'Mechanism operates a flood-unit which is irreversible. After operation, personnel have ten minutes to clear the area before flooding is complete.'

Dryden turned to Pryderi and Stigand.

'I think everything is in order,' he said. 'Cador and I will go on to Level Seven and start the destruct mechanisms. You wait for us here.'

He motioned Cador to follow him into the elevator. Within moments they were back on Level Seven. Dryden did not prevaricate. He went straight to the control panel.

'Pray to Bel that this mechanism still works, Cador,' he said grimly as he read the instructions once again.

'I do not understand what is happening, Yaghus,' returned Cador, 'but I trust your plan works.'

Dryden flicked several switches, and then pressed a red button. Everything on the control panel remained dead.

His heart sank.

He returned the switches to their former positions and re-read the instructions.

Ah! He had not pressed the master-switch which activated the entire panel. He pulled down the lever indicated. There was a coughing sound and then a steady hum. Cador stared in surprise. Swiftly Dryden repeated the sequences of flicking switches.

Somewhere - it seemed miles away - there was a muffled roar and the ground began to tremble beneath their feet.

Dryden turned to Cador with a raised eyebrow.

'It's worked,' he said shortly. 'Let's get out of here!'

Thaec, Faeder of the Cynn, heard the muffled roar and felt the shake of the ground beneath his feet. In fact, it caused the glass in his hand to shake and some of the liquid to spill on his uniform. He frowned.

'What is that?' he demanded of the *weardian* who stood at rigid attention by the door of the room.

'I do not know, *mín* Faeder,' replied the man.

Thaec shrugged and turned away but, a moment later, Wulfnoth burst unceremoniously into the room. His face was ghastly white.

'Thaec - *mín* Faeder' - !

Thaec stared at the *eorl* in astonishment.

'What do you mean by ...' he began in a stentorian voice.

'We must evacuate this level at once,' interrupted Wulfnoth, hysteria in his voice. 'There has been some sort of explosion. There is water flooding into the level everywhere. They think it is the water tanks - the level is flooding - flooding rapidly!'

Thaec stared at Wulfnoth aghast.

'How long to evacuate?' he whispered.

Aelmihtig knows, *mín* Faeder! You must get out immediately. I do not think there is long.'

'Quickly then. To the elevators!' Panic edged the Faeder's voice.

He turned and started running from his apartments. Outside, in the thoroughfares of Level Seven, screaming people were running to and fro. Wulfnoth, trying to follow Thaec, was cut off almost immediately and went down beneath a stampeding crowd. A small body of *weardian* formed a close knot around their Faeder and began to fight their way through to the elevators. A phalanx of guards was holding back the people from one elevator reserved for the Faeder. Thaec and his men forced their way through and the door slid shut behind them.

'To the next level!' snapped Thaec, wiping the sweat from his brow.

They had hardly started upwards when another roar came to

158

their ears and the elevator paused dramatically in its smooth upward journey, rocking dangerously before continuing. One of the guards spoke rapidly into the communication panel and then turned to Thaec with a startled face.

'Level Six reports a similar explosion. The water tanks are flooding that level, *mín* Faeder!'

'What?' cried Thaec. 'Take the elevator all the way up to the surface. Then have the entire See-ti evacuated!'

When Dryden and Cador reached Level Three, the first of the slave levels, the sounds of pandemonium came clearly to their ears. Pryderi and Stigand were waiting for them impatiently.

'Right,' snapped Dryden, as he left the elevator, 'we must fight our way to the speaker system so that Stigand has his chance to warn the slaves. What the Cynn may not realise is that Levels Three to One are perfectly safe until we operate the destructor mechanism. They may be already panicking and, if so, we'll be able to use that as a distraction.'

As they passed from the Forbidden Zone into the warm green expanse of the 'yeast culture fields' where the food harvests were constantly grown and collected, Dryden found that he had made an understatement. Groups of slaves stood here and there huddled in bewildered groups while black uniformed guards were running in panic for the elevators. Stigand shouted to the nearest group of slaves and they broke up and began to run in several directions.

'I have told them to tell all the others. They must evacuate to the surface,' gasped Stigand. 'But we must get to the speaker.'

The four of them raced through the alleyways between the yeast troughs, mixing with running slaves and panicking *weardian*. Once they saw three slaves attack a *weardian* and snatch his weapon from his belt, killing him within the moment. Chaos reigned everywhere: screams, shouts and curses filled the air.

Then they were at the control panels - mostly deserted now. One guard still stood resolutely trying to keep the people away but Dryden launched himself at the man, grabbing for his weapon. As it fell from his hand, Pryderi grabbed it and began to use it as a club. Dryden rendered the guard unconscious with a swift blow to the jaw.

'The speaker system, Stigand? Where is it?' gasped Dryden.

'Here!' cried the old man, throwing himself into a chair at the control panel. He pulled forward what was obviously a microphone and began jabbing at switches. Then he began to speak rapidly into the instrument. Dryden could hear his words echoing across the level. He spoke first in the language of the Cynn and then in *Kernewek*.

'Slaves of the See-ti! Slaves on all levels! The See-ti is being destroyed! I repeat - the See-ti is being destroyed! Already levels seven to four are under water. Levels three, two and one will soon be submerged. Flee for your lives, flee to the elevators and escape to the surface. Liberty is now yours. The Cynn are destroyed!'

Two guards came racing towards them, unslinging their weapons. Before they had time to use them Pryderi and Cador had closed upon them. Cador still retained his long sword and felled one easily while Pryderi swung his makeshift club into the face of the other.

'I think that is it, Yaghus,' cried the old man. 'I have broadcast to all the levels. There is nothing more I can do now.'

'Back to the Forbidden Zone then,' said Dryden.

It took some minutes for them to traverse the yeast fields, back through the now deserted avenues of yeast troughs, and then up into the passage that led to the Forbidden Zone. Within moments they had carried out the self-destruct ritual and were speeding towards Level Two.

It was then that Stigand gave a groan of pain.

'What's the matter, old man,' cried Pryderi. 'Are you wounded?'

'No. But the force field - I forgot the force field!'

'What do you mean?'

'On Level One ... for the slaves to escape the force field needs to be turned off.'

Dryden swore.

Stigand was right. It was no good urging the slaves to escape if they were locked in by the force field.

'Very well,' he said curtly. 'Before we destroy Level One we must get the force field turned off.'

They passed rapidly through Level Two, pausing just long enough for Dryden to activate the switches. Then, at Level One, they entered the great gloomy cavern where the slave compounds were. They

160

could hear the terrible noise of wailing and crying as the slaves stood helpless within their compounds, cut off by the force field, and thinking they had been left alone to die. All the guards had deserted. Some of the slaves, in desperation, had attempted to get through the force field and their bodies lay in huddled masses.

Dryden and his companions ran along the side of the male compound towards the control buildings. Seeing them, the slaves set up a great shouting, pleading with them to free them. There was no time to give them assurances.

'Where would the force field controls be, Stigand?' Dryden snapped.

Stigand, gasping at his side, pointed to the towers at the main gate. It seemed so long ago that Dryden had passed between their portals as a prisoner.

'In there, Yaghus. The controls for both female and male compounds are there.'

The four of them burst into the buildings. In a small room they found a series of controls but Dryden could not read the signs that labelled them. Stigand moved forward, paused and then began turning off switches.

'I think that does it, Yaghus,' he grunted.

'Let's go,' snapped Dryden.

Outside a veritable sea of slaves, freed from their confinement, was rushing towards the elevators. Dryden and his companions had difficulty dodging through them and making their way back towards the Forbidden Zone.

'That was easy,' smiled Pryderi as they hurried through the tunnels. 'The guards must have completely deserted!'

'I only hope the majority will be able to get up to the surface,' murmured Stigand.

Dryden pushed them towards the elevator.

'Get in. I'll activate the destruct mechanism.'

He bent over the switches. They hummed and his finger hovered over the button.

There was a shout from the corridor. Dryden whirled to find two *weardian* bursting into the chamber with levelled guns. He heard an explosion and felt the hot blast from one of their weapons sting close by his face. Cador, standing at the entrance of the lift, suddenly gave a cry and launched himself at the men. There was a flash from the second man's weapon, aimed at Dryden, but it was Cador who took the impact. He staggered back a little and then, as if summoning up a hidden strength, pushed himself forward, his hands closing on the *weardian's* throat. They fell back together.

Dryden leapt forward, kicking out at the first guard. Pryderi was coming to his aid, grabbing at Cador's longsword and swinging it at the first guard, who was trying to fire again. The guard used his weapon to parry the blows but it was an unequal contest. Within seconds he fell, pierced through the chest. Pryderi turned as Dryden bent to help Cador. But Cador's assailant was lying still, his head at an unusual angle.

They bent and helped Cador to his feet. His shirt was stained with blood seeping from an open wound in his shoulder.

'Does it hurt much?' asked Dryden.

Cador smiled thinly.

'Nothing that can't be mended, healer. Maybe you can mend me as you mended the slaves of Lan-Howlek and patched their wounds?'

Dryden frowned.

'You remember?'

Cador breathed in with a wheezing sigh. It was obvious that he was in pain in spite of his great control.

'I started to remember down there - down in the sewers, just after we met up with you. My memory has been back some time now, Yaghus of Lan-Kern.'

His eyes suddenly rolled back and he fainted.

'Quickly,' wailed Stigand. 'They may be sending other guards after us.'

Pryderi dragged Cador's unconscious form into the lift while Dryden operated the destruct mechanism and followed him.

They reached the small ante-chamber and managed to climb up through the hole in the roof into the open air. Kigva, Onnen and Elgiva were waiting for them. Onnen gave a wail of anguish as she saw Dryden and Pryderi bringing Cador through the aperture but Dryden tried to reassure her.

'It's only a flesh wound, Onnen. Don't worry. He will be all right with a little attention.'

162

Under Dryden's direction they carried him into the shelter of the trees and laid him by the stream. Onnen tore off Cador's sticky, blood-stained shirt and began to wash the wound.

Stigand was telling Elgiva what had happened but there was little need for those who had remained on the surface to ask whether the attempt had been successful. Across the vast plain, under which the See-ti had been constructed, they had heard muffled roaring sounds and felt the ground shaking as if prey to some tremendous earthquake. Dryden could see in the gloom of early evening groups of people straggling across the great plain, wandering to and fro as if in a daze. There were only a few black-clad figures among them. Most of them were in the slave garb of the See-ti.

Dryden nodded approvingly at Stigand.

'Well, old man, at least you have caused some of the people to be saved ... some of the innocent, anyway.'

'I will go and speak to them,' Stigand said. 'I will try to find out what has happened and what can be done now. They will need some organisation if they are to survive in this inhospitable world.'

'I'll come with you,' said Pryderi as Stigand began to walk off.

Dryden turned back to the unconscious form of Cador. Kigva was gazing down at him with a curious expression on her face while Onnen was cradling the man's head in her arms. The blonde-haired girl looked up at Dryden with a tear-stained face.

'Can't you do anything for him?' she asked.

Dryden peered round at the undergrowth and spotted an oak tree.

'Onnen, you start a fire going. Help her Elgiva. Kigva - take Onnen's knife and fetch me the young bark and the leaves of that oak tree.'

For a moment Kigva looked as if she would refuse Dryden's order. Then she shrugged, took Onnen's knife and went to perform the task.

The knife blade was red hot. Dryden waited until it cooled a little. Cador was conscious now, looking up at Dryden curiously.

'I have to remove the projectile from your shoulder,' Dryden told him. 'It will hurt.'

The man nodded and turned his head. At a gesture from Dryden, Onnen leant forward and grasped his hands. He moaned slightly as

Dryden probed for the bullet. Then he felt it, and began to draw it up. Cador slumped into a merciful unconsciousness. Having taken the tiny piece of metal from the flesh, Dryden turned to the mash of oak bark and leaves he had prepared and applied it to the wound.

'It will staunch the blood and facilitate the healing,' he said, forcing a smile at Onnen. 'Don't worry, he will be all right.'

Onnen tried to return the smile through her tears.

Kigva watched in silence. As Dryden turned away, she followed him.

'I cannot understand it, Yaghus,' she hissed, when they passed out of earshot of Onnen. 'After what that man has done to you in the past, what he has done to me and my family, you try to save him!'

'He saved my life down there,' said Dryden shortly.

'An evil will never become a good,' snapped Kigva as she turned and strode away to join Elgiva, sitting by the fire. Dryden stared after her and sighed. He heard a noise close by and turned to find Onnen watching him.

'Yaghus,' she said slowly. 'I will not let anyone harm Cador. I do not know what harm he has done you, Pryderi or Kigva. I know that once he was an evil man but he is not evil now, and I - I love him!'

Dryden nodded.

'Yes, Onnen, I know it.'

'And no one shall harm him,' repeated the girl. 'No one.'

'Yaghus!'

It was Stigand returning with Pryderi. They seemed excited and their faces were animated.

'The entire See-ti is apparently under water,' began Pryderi. 'All the levels are flooded - most of the Cynn are drowned!'

'They have rescued little from the debacle,' nodded Stigand. 'All the flying machines have been lost and most of their weapons. There are only a few groups here and there that are armed and those are totally demoralised.'

'Did Thaec perish on Level Seven?' asked Dryden.

Stigand shrugged.

'No one knows, not for certain. There were apparently no survivors from the lower levels. A number of *weardian* survived from the slave levels and, as near as we can estimate, some fifteen hundred men and women from the slave levels have survived.'

164

Dryden plucked at his lower lip.

'That is not many compared with the numbers that were there,' he said.

'The survivors have asked Stigand to become their leader,' went on Pryderi, trying to overcome the awkward pause. 'They've asked him to form a committee to organise a camp. Very few of the surviving slaves want to go back to their former countries - the *morlader*, those of Lan-Kern or Lan-Howlek. They have been away too long. They and the Cynn slaves want Stigand to lead them in establishing a new settlement.'

'That is an excellent idea,' approved Dryden.

Stigand spread his hands.

'It is too early for them to know their own minds,' he said. 'And anyway, when they are finally in a position to make their choice without emotional influence then there are probably others more qualified to lead them than an old man like me.'

'But in the meantime they want Stigand to lead them,' smiled Pryderi.

'I have asked them to let me have until morning to think about it.'

Dryden grinned.

'It is always better to make a decision of moment after some sleep.'

'And we can sleep peacefully now. The world is safe from Thaec and his hordes,' Pryderi sighed. 'Bel be thanked for that.'

CHAPTER FOUR

Night descended across the great plain. The camp fires of the former slaves of the Cynn caused a reddish glow to illuminate the plain and turn inquisitive animals back into the surrounding forests. At the edge of one section of forest some dark figures stirred. They were not denizens of the wild but men - men who shunned the friendly fires and the warmth of their fellow humans - men who moved cautiously through the undergrowth and gazed malevolently at the rejoicing people as they camped in their new-found freedom.

Thaec scowled into the night.

'Vermin!' he hissed as he took in the flickering fires.

'Shall we attack, *mín* Faeder?' asked one of the men at his side.

'Attack?' snorted Thaec. 'Attack? *Dumb-héafod!* There are but six of us and hundreds of them. Attack?'

'Surely there must be more of the Cynn who escaped?' whispered another man, aghast.

'Where are they, *weardian*?' demanded Thaec. 'Where are our armies?'

He blinked at the fires again.

'Yet we will have our vengeance, never fear. By the *Aelmihtig*, I have sworn it!'

'Vengeance?' ventured the guard.

'Vengeance on the outlander who reduced us to this state,' returned Thaec bitterly. 'Oh yes, it was the outlander, Dryden, who destroyed us. I am certain of that. He was too cunning. I underestimated him. But I shall have revenge.'

No one dared to ask the inevitable question of the Faeder and Thaec appeared to be unaware of their questioning gaze.

'The outlander shall pay dearly. We will wait. We will watch. There will come a time when he and his companions will be separated from the rest of these vermin. Then we shall strike!'

166

'Well, Stigand,' Dryden said as they gathered the next morning, 'and have you decided what you will do?'

The old man looked at the chaos about them; at the hundreds of former slaves huddled across the plain, at his daughter's face turned towards him.

'Yes, Yaghus. If they want me as a leader, I am prepared to serve until they find someone more suitable. Many of them,' he nodded to the ex-slaves, 'are outlanders who will need little assistance as they resume their former ways of life. Others, the Cynn, will need to adjust carefully to life on the surface. I have already issued orders that those with eye shades must wear them during the daylight hours while those who do not must bandage their eyes from the light. They will gradually become adapted.'

'Have you decided how you will exist?'

Stigand smiled.

'There are many former hunters and farmers among the outlander slaves. We can try to organise a farming community and get some to teach the others their skills. I think we will survive.'

He paused and smiled at Dryden.

'You would be most welcome to stay with us. You, Yaghus, more than I deserve the honour of leading these people. You are truly their saviour.'

Dryden shook his head.

'We must return to Lan-Kern soon. I have fulfilled one of my quests,' he smiled gently at the dark-haired girl, 'but I still have another to pursue.'

'That shouldn't be difficult, Yaghus,' interrupted Pryderi, who stood with them, 'now that Cador has recovered his memory.'

Dryden turned to where Cador was lying, his back supported by a tree trunk, being attended by Onnen.

'Ay, Cador,' he muttered.

Pryderi glanced at Dryden anxiously.

'He saved your life, Yaghus, at cost to himself.'

'Yet there is still the question of his crimes to be answered,' Dryden pointed out.

'Each man is the prisoner of his environment,' said Stigand suddenly. 'Few men create the circumstances of their life, most of them merely react to those circumstances. Would Thaec have been evil if he was not raised among evil?'

Pryderi clapped the old man on the shoulder.

'Spoken as a true *drewyth*, friend Stigand.'

'Yes,' persisted Dryden. 'Thaec was an evil man. But you, Stigand - you were also raised among the Cynn. Yet you did not succumb to such moral degeneration. A man's environment cannot be blamed for all his actions.'

'But it must be taken into account, Yaghus,' insisted Pryderi. 'Not all men react in the same way in similar circumstances, that is true, but all men are marked by those circumstances.'

Dryden looked closely at his young friend.

'Do you defend Cador? He slew your brother Peredur, your cousin Teyrnon, he kidnapped Kigva and stole *An Kevryn* from Meneghy.'

Pryderi held up his hand.

'The list of his crimes is long. Yet I still adhere to the teaching of the *drewyth*. No matter what evil a man does he can still expiate that evil. In my eyes Cador has won a new chance in life.'

He nodded towards Onnen as she bathed Cador's face.

'I think he has a good chance now, perhaps the only chance he has ever had, to make a positive contribution to life.'

Dryden turned to Kigva. The girl looked at her brother Pryderi with troubled eyes.

'No person who has suffered emotional and physical wrong at the hands of another should be asked to pronounce judgement on them. Emotion will always overrule logic and justice. You cannot expect me to hate and despise Cador one day and forgive him the next day? I shall despise him always. The events are too close for me to see them in the moral perspective which the *drewyth* say should temper our justice. So do not ask me to contribute to this discussion.'

'The decision is yours, Yaghus,' said Pryderi.

Dryden turned and walked to where Cador lay. Onnen looked up and an anxious frown creased her brow.

'He is still weak from the loss of blood,' she said defensively.

Cador looked up at Dryden and a faint flush came to his cheeks.

'It is all right, Onnen,' he said quietly. He regarded Dryden thoughtfully for a moment and then grimaced ruefully. 'I know what is in your mind, Yaghus. I remember all my past life as well as these few days since I met Onnen and came to the See-ti. My life in Lan-Howlek was not a life to be proud of. I undersand that. Will you take me back to Dynas Drok for trial?'

Onnen turned pale and clenched her hands.

'They will surely kill him,' she whispered.

Dryden squatted by Cador's side.

'That is not the way of the *drewyth*,' he corrected. 'Cunobel, who now rules Lan-Howlek under the High Chieftainship of Kesmur of Lan-Kern, believes most strongly in the moral code of the *drewyth*. Death is an easy retribution in which those who exact judicial murder sink to the level of the criminal.'

'So you *are* taking him back?' demanded Onnen.

Dryden did not answer immediately. He looked deeply into Cador's eyes.

'I have my life to thank you for, Cador.'

The former warlord of Lan-Howlek shrugged and nodded to his shoulder.

'A debt swiftly repaid,' he answered.

'Do you regret your past life?'

Cador sighed.

'Repent or regret? Don't we all regret and repent the vanished past, wanting to live our lives over again? But in the sense you mean it, I would be less than honest if I were to tell you that I did. A man does not change his nature in a single night. But this I will say - I was a spoilt and indolent youth. It was easy for me to adopt the role my mother, Logosen, and my grandmother, Nelferch, pressed upon me from my cradle. I will not say that I had no choice in the matter. But I was lazy and the path was easy. In the light of circumstances, in the light of the suffering I witnessed in the See-ti, I wish I could have lived a different life. But I did not. There is an end to it. I have wronged a great many people. It is therefore just that I return to answer for my misdeeds.'

'No!' the cry was wrested from Onnen. It was a cry of pain. 'No,' she whispered. 'I was taught to hate Cador of Lan-Howlek for the evil that he and his family did to my people. But in the forests I came to know a man called Cad who behaved honourably and was brave. I came to love that man. And Cador is still the man I knew in the forest whether he be Cad or Cador!'

Cador smiled painfully. 'We are prisoners of our past, Onnen.'

Dryden felt disconcerted as he looked at them. Suddenly a resolution began to form in his mind.

'What would you do if you were free to do as you like, Cador?' he asked.

Cador glanced up swiftly, trying to read what lay behind Dryden's words.

'I would go north to the coast of Lan-Howlek and, if Onnen would have me, help her to rebuild the settlement of her father which was destroyed by the *morlader*. I would try to farm and work the land there.'

Onnen bent forward and gripped Cador's hand in her own.

'*If* I would have you, Cador? You must know that I would.'

'And you would be content to live under the rule of Cunobel?' persisted Dryden. 'You would not nurture hatred at the death of Nelferch or the downfall of your mother Logosen?'

'I have learned much in these last few days, Yaghus. More than I ever did in my misspent youth. I would try to expiate my former life by creation and not by destruction.'

Dryden nodded.

'If it is the wish of you both to start such a life, Cador, then I will not stop you.'

Cador looked at Dryden in disbelief. Onnen, overcome with emotion, grasped at Dryden's hand and kissed it.

'You are truly one with Bel, Yaghus. Thank you,' she cried.

'There is a payment,' Dryden said gruffly, getting to his feet.

Cador looked suspiciously at him. 'Payment?'

'Now that your memory has returned, Cador, you will recall what you did with *An Kevryn*. It is my mission to take it back to the *drewyth* sanctuary at Meneghy.'

'*An Kevryn*?' Cador started. 'I'd almost forgotten.'

He smiled broadly. 'Yes, Yaghus, I can recall where I hid *An Kevryn*.'

'Can you direct me there?'

'Even better. If you can wait a day until my wound heals a little more, I shall take you there,' replied Cador. 'It was a place near to where I first met Onnen, a small cave by the bank of a stream.

From there, Onnen and I can go northward.'

Dryden smiled.

'Lead me to *An Kevryn*,' he vowed, 'and you can go where you wish.'

'Bel will bless you for this, Yaghus,' smiled Onnen.

Dryden shrugged.

'We will start out in a day or two, Cador, when you are better.'

CHAPTER FIVE

The sun was high in a brilliant blue, cloudless sky when they gathered to say goodbye to Stigand and Elgiva. The old man and his daughter solemnly shook each of them by the hand. Stigand was blinking too rapidly, to belie the fact that tears lay just beneath the surface.

'I wish you would stay, Yaghus,' he said sadly. 'I wish you would all stay.'

Dryden smiled warmly. 'You'll make out, Stigand. Of that I'm sure.'

'Yes,' agreed Pryderi. 'Soon you'll have a thriving community here.'

The old man looked hesitantly from Pryderi to Dryden.

'It was best that the Cynn and their philosophies should perish. Only out of that destruction could we begin to recreate a healthy society. Isn't that so?'

'It is so, Stigand. You will be building for Elgiva's future - for her and for others like her.'

Elgiva smiled. 'I know that you will return to us one day, Yaghus.'

Cador and Onnen, Dryden, Pryderi and Kigva shouldered their bags containing food for the journey. Amongst the debris from the See-ti a number of outlander swords and javelins had been found and the three men had equipped themselves for the dangerous journey through the great forests to the west. They turned to wave to Stigand and Elgiva and then marched without a further word across the great plain under which the ruined See-ti now lay.

They travelled for some time before entering the gloomy forests. They had no horses to speed their journey but they walked with a light step for each step brought them nearer to their homes.

Cador and Onnen stayed slightly apart from the others. Kigva refused to have any dealings with Cador and while Onnen could rationally appreciate Kigva's attitude, having suffered such wrong at Cador's hands, she felt emotionally resentful. Dryden, too, did not feel entirely at ease in the new circumstances. He could not fail to recall the attempts Cador had made to kill him during the grim battles in Dynas Drok, Nelferch's aptly named Fortress of Evil. It was difficult to reconcile the Cador of old with the man who had saved his life in the See-ti. Suspicion was a natural thing to feel. Yet Dryden had reached a decision about Cador and he was prepared to stick to that decision.

Only Pryderi behaved to any degree in a natural way. Dryden ascribed this to the young man's training as a *drewyth* and the depth of his belief in the *drewyth* philosophy that man was not all bad or all good but a mixture of the two, and that circumstances alone unchained that aspect which was to dominate. The philosophy taught the concept that punishment was a negative force. If one transgressed moral or community law then one should be given the opportunity to redeem oneself and contribute to society to compensate for those transgressions. Compensation and rehabilitation were the very basis of Lan-Kern's way of dealing with wrongdoers. In Pryderi's eyes Cador had gone a long way towards redeeming himself.

On the journey westward Dryden found himself becoming more and more awkward in the presence of Kigva. There seemed to arise a slight distance between them. Following their escape from the See-ti, Dryden had become awkward and almost tongue-tied in her presence. He recalled that when he had first confessed his love for her - back in those quiet days before Kigva had been abducted from Lan-Kern - she had rebuked him and informed him that she was to marry Teyrnon, the warlord of Lan-Kern. But subsequently Teyrnon had been killed defending Meneghy from the raiders of Lan-Howlek. Dryden now wondered whether to remind the girl of his avowal of love. Would she greet it with scorn and derision?

With such thoughts troubling him, Dryden became silent and brooding. It was Pryderi who began to take over the leadership of their party as they moved through the towering conifers and dense undergrowth of the great forests. Cador and Onnen thought his brooding silence was directed towards them, but Pryderi appreciated the delicate relationship between the man he admired and called friend, and his sister. Yet with all his *drewyth* wisdom he was at a

173

loss as to how to approach the problem.

During one halt it was Onnen who approached Dryden.

'As soon as Cador has shown you where he hid *An Kevryn*, we will turn northwards to the coast and that will be the last you will see of us.'

Dryden glanced up at the aggressive tone in the girl's voice.

'Very well,' he replied, wondering what had caused her obvious ill-humour.

'Do not worry, Yaghus,' the girl went on, 'Cador will not trouble you again. You will have no cause to regret your decision to let us lead new lives of our own making.'

'I have no doubt of that,' answered Dryden. Then he realised what was prompting the girl's attitude. He was immediately contrite and cursed himself for his selfish behaviour. At the same time he decided he would have to talk with Kigva. He waited until they had made camp and the others were engaged in preparations for the night before following Kigva to where she sat, slightly apart, before a pool which was fed by a softly gurgling stream.

'I have to speak with you, Kigva,' he began awkwardly.

She glanced up and inclined her head. Dryden sat down by the girl and gazed silently into the blackness of the pool for a while. He was silent for so long that she glanced swiftly at him out of the corner of her eye, sensing his difficulty in forming words.

'Soon we will be back in Lan-Kern, Kigva,' he said slowly.

'I look forward to it, Yaghus. It seems an eternity since I was captured at Meneghy.'

'Kigva,' Dryden's voice was unnaturally harsh. 'I must talk with you ...'

She could not suppress a gentle grin.

'You are talking with me, Yaghus.'

'I find this more difficult to say each time,' he went on. 'Once I spoke to you at Dynas Dor - once I told you that I love you.'

'I remember it,' the girl bowed her head.

'You were pledged to Teyrnon then.'

'I remember,' the girl repeated.

'I - I just wanted to say that nothing has changed for me since then. I still love you, Kigva.'

Dryden looked fixedly at the pool of water.

174

Kigva heaved a deep sigh.

'There is no need to tell you that I feel much for you, Yaghus. Tenderness and sincere friendship.'

There was a silence.

'Yaghus - we have been through much together, you and I. I told you once, long ago, that I do not know the meaning of this word "love". To me it is an unreal thing, the romance which the bards sing and speak about is, to me a mysticism which I cannot share.'

'Love is a reality, Kigva,' there was pain in his voice.

'Love is a shadowy force,' replied the girl, with a shake of her raven black hair. 'The only reason a person loves is for his own pleasure. I want no person to love me - it creates obligations and I cannot love in return and fulfil those obligations.'

Dryden felt a tremendous ache in his chest and he stood up.

'Wait, Yaghus,' cried the girl, grabbing his hand. 'Tell me this, do you feel you love me because you need me?'

Dryden shook his head.

'I need you because I love you,' he replied.

Kigva smiled wistfully.

'It appears to me, Yaghus, that this love you speak of has one arch-enemy.'

'What is that?' frowned Dryden.

'Life itself,' replied the girl.

'Did you love Teyrnon?' he demanded suddenly.

Anger clouded the girl's eyes for a moment and then she forced her features to relax.

'I told you before, Yaghus, that "love" is an unknown concept for me. For poor Teyrnon I had a great regard. I respected him and there were bonds of familiarity between us. We grew up together and I felt close friendship and tenderness for him. The custom of my people required that I should marry and Teyrnon was a natural choice. I have never "loved", Yaghus. Not then - not now. Teyrnon is now dead and I know he did you a great wrong. Let the dead now remain dead.'

Red-faced at this gentle rebuke Dryden turned away from Kigva's unhappy eyes.

'One moment more, Yaghus.'

He halted.

175

'I cannot return your love. But friendship, tenderness, concern, these things I do feel for you. I do not want you to be unhappy. But I cannot admit to an emotion I do not feel. If there is one man apart from my father or my brother Pryderi that I truly care about, then it is you, Yaghus. Please do not go away unhappy.'

Dryden turned a little.

'Remember, Kigva, that I love you,' he mumbled, feeling foolish.

The girl smiled at his solemn face.

'I'll remember, Yaghus,' she answered.

For three more days they journeyed on through the forest. Dryden tried to make up for his previous selfishness and to weld the party together in preparation for the dangers ahead. Although the See-ti flying machines were now destroyed, there were other threats of danger from the *gourgath*, the *morlader* or a hundred and one forest dwellers. Dryden urged the party forward and tried to instil in the others a new zest for their journey.

It is impossible to say what Dryden's thoughts would have been had he known that barely a mile behind him there strode a file of black clad figures. At their head, anger distorting his otherwise handsome face, strode Thaec, Faeder of the Cynn, while behind him came six men all dressed in the uniforms of the *weardian*. They halted in a small clearing and one of the guards dropped to his knees to examine the ground.

'They halted here a while, *mín* Faeder,' he said. 'They cannot be very far ahead of us now.'

Thaec smiled grimly.

'Then we shall go on immediately.'

The guard frowned.

'The men are exhausted, *mín* Faeder,' he protested hesitantly. 'Shouldn't we try to rest here?'

'We shall go on immediately,' said Thaec with a snarl. 'Another march and we shall catch them - catch that accursed outlander.'

The *weardian* pointed to the weapons they carried.

'But, *mín* Faeder, there is very little ammunition left. If we shared it out I doubt whether we would have one shot apiece.'

Thaec turned on the man and swore.

'That does not matter. The outlander swine are armed only with their heathen knives anyway. Let us have enough of these whines,

176

weardian. We shall press on and overtake them. Do you hear? The outlanders must pay for their destruction of the Cynn!'

Onnen looked about her in bewilderment. They had halted on the edge of a clearing.

'But this was the clearing in which the *morlader* camped before we were attacked by the flying machine of the See-ti. But ... but where are the bodies of those who died at the hands of the Cynn?'

Cador was nodding in agreement.

'Onnen is right. This is the same clearing.'

'We know,' said Dryden. 'Pryderi and I found a man still alive here, although he only lived long enough to tell us what had happened.'

Pryderi moved forward.

'The weapons of the *morlader* are still here, Yaghus, and pieces of their clothing and ...'

He halted, staring at the ground.

'*Gourgath*?' Cador commented laconically.

Pryderi pursed his lips .

'So much for the mystery. Their bodies have become meals for the scavengers.'

Kigva shivered. 'Let us move on.'

'Which way, Cador?' Dryden asked as they hurried across the clearing.

'Over this way,' responded Cador. 'I came into the clearing from this direction. Not far away there should be a small stream, somewhere along which I hid *An Kevryn* for safe keeping and in order that I might travel more quickly.'

It took them over an hour to walk along the small forest path and to find the stream. Cador took some minutes to get his bearings and then he turned excitedly.

'It's not far now. The cave entrance is just a few hundred yards away.'

Sure enough, having followed the stream for a short distance, Cador paused at a bracken covered bank and pointed.

'The cave entrance is here.'

Dryden saw him frowning at the bracken.

'What is it, Cador?' he asked. 'Is anything wrong?'

'The bracken is broken and bent,' Cador replied hesitantly. 'I took great trouble to disguise the entrance of the cave.'

'Perhaps a storm or some animal has crushed the bracken?' suggested Pryderi.

But Cador was already pushing through the undergrowth towards the hidden cave entrance. The others waited expectantly on the bank of the stream. Cador had only to glance inside the cave to confirm the truth of his suspicion.

He turned back, his face pale.

'*An Kevryn*,' he said slowly. 'It's gone!'

CHAPTER SIX

'Gone?'

Dryden stared aghast at Cador.

'Yes, Yaghus. I placed it just within the cave mouth - buried it. But someone has dug it up. It is gone.'

Pryderi was bending down to examine the ground in the cave mouth.

'There are signs of two men here. See in the soft sand? There are the marks of Cador's feet but look closer, there and there. Those are larger imprints - a person wearing a curious footwear that I think is unknown in these parts.'

'Who?' demanded Cador.

With a grunt, Pryderi stooped to retrieve something from the ground. It was a broad-bladed knife, the instrument the person who had taken *An Kevryn* had apparently used to dig it up. It was curiously ornamented.

'*Morlader!*'

Dryden frowned.

'But there was no sign of *An Kevryn* among the slain *morlader*. Are you saying that the Cynn carried it off?'

Onnen shook her head.

'They did not have the box with them, Yaghus. But -' Suddenly her eyes grew round. 'Wait! There was one of the *morlader* who ... The *morlader* caught me at a spot not far from here and then made camp in the clearing we have just left. It was nearly dusk but one of their number went off into the forest - to hunt, I think. He never came back. We thought that the Cynn had carried him off. I seem to recall the *morlader* calling his name. What was it? He was a tall, black-bearded man.'

'Conla!'

They turned to Cador.

'When I came upon the *morlader* they were calling for him,' explained Cador. 'They were crying the name Conla.'

'If the *morlader*, Conla, did take it, where did he go?'

Onnen shrugged.

'Back to the *morlader* ships on the northern coast?'

'Then we must follow.'

'You will go nowhere, outlander!' The voice was harsh and familiar.

They froze like statues as six black uniformed figures emerged from the surrounding undergrowth, each of them with a levelled weapon in his hand. Slowly Dryden turned and faced the grimly smiling leader who had spoken.

'Thaec,' he said, his voice catching in his throat.

'Yes, outlander,' replied the Faeder of the Cynn. 'You did not think that you could destroy me that easily, did you?'

'Rats are not easily drowned,' replied Pryderi, his mouth tight.

'Silence, vermin!' snarled the Faeder in his direction. 'Death will come to you quickly or slowly, just as your conduct merits. But as for you, outlander,' he turned to face Dryden with a mocking leer and raised his gun. 'I will enjoy this task.'

Dryden saw the Cynn's finger whitening as the knuckle began to exert its pressure on the trigger. In sheer desperation he launched himself towards Thaec. He felt the blast of the weapon and a stinging on his shoulder. Then he struck the man in the chest and Thaec toppled backwards.

Around him Dryden was conscious of the cries of his companions, the ring of swords and discharge of Cynn weapons.

Thaec had dropped his gun and was now clawing at Dryden's throat, seeking a strangle-hold.

Dryden swung a fist into the side of the man's face, causing him to grunt in pain. But Thaec was a strong man. He flung Dryden from him and stooped to recover his gun. He had time only to catch hold of it as a club before Dryden was attacking again. Thaec made several vicious swings at Dryden's head but Dryden dodged and ducked, avoiding the weapon.

Now Dryden had his sword out and was moving forward for another attack, swinging his blade to counter Thaec's makeshift club and seeking to get under the Faeder's guard.

180

He became aware of another black uniformed figure coming to Thaec's aid and of someone else closing with the man. In the corner of his eye, the two figures blurred into one, going down together. Dryden pulled his eyes back to concentrate on Thaec but the second's distraction had given the Faeder of the Cynn the opportunity to raise his weapon and Dryden knew that it was useless to fight further. Thaec's finger was already closing on the trigger.

Dryden felt his body tense and his eyes shut automatically to take the blast of the weapon.

No blast came. Instead there was a gulping cough and Dryden opened his eyes. Thaec was standing before him, his weapon lowered, his eyes large and round, staring in surprise.

From his chest, squarely above his heart, the handle of a dagger stood out, a red stain spreading from it. Thaec coughed again, blood spurting from his mouth. Then he sank to his knees, fell forward on his face and lay still.

Dryden, mesmerised by the sight, finally pulled himself together and turned. Kigva, pale-faced, stood staring at the body of Thaec, shuddering. Dryden sprang to her side and swept an arm around her. He became aware that six black uniformed figures lay sprawled by the banks of the stream. Pryderi and Cador stood there, with their chests heaving and blood-stained swords in their hands. Onnen stood by Cador, a knife in her hand. For a moment no one said anything, staring at the scene of carnage.

Finally Pryderi cleared his throat and pointed.

'These others - fools! Their weapons were useless.'

'Useless?' Dryden queried.

He moved forward and picked up one of the guns of the Cynn. It was obvious that there was no ammunition in it. Puzzled, he made a swift check of the other guns. Only Thaec's weapon and one other had the Cynn equivalent of bullets.

'We did not know they were weaponless,' muttered Pryderi defensively. 'We need not have killed them.'

'They came at us as if they were armed,' agreed Cador.

'It is no one's fault,' observed Dryden, 'except possibly the fault of their culture. Blind obedience, that's what it was. The Faeder's orders had to be obeyed.'

He gazed down at Thaec's body.

'At least we now know that Thaec is dead.'

Cador was examining one of the Cynn weapons.

'Perhaps we can learn the secret of these things? With such weapons we would not have to fear any attacks on our people.'

Pryderi gave a shudder. Swiftly, before their astonished gaze, he gathered all six weapons and flung them in the deepest part of the stream.

'This world is not ready for such instruments of death and I pray Bel that it never will be.'

'What do you mean, Pryderi?' asked Onnen.

The young *drewyth's* face was animated.

'As I understand it, the Cynn believed they were a superior civilisation at least partly because they were possessed of such instruments of death. How long would it be before our people, forsaking the way of Bel, having such weapons, would begin to feel themselves superior to all others?'

'Pryderi is right,' agreed Dryden. 'In my world people measured the greatness of their civilisation by the sophistication of their weapons and by the amount of territory they were able to control, empires were thought of as badges of civilised greatness. Countries that possessed art, literature and philosophy but no empires or armies were regarded as backward and unsophisticated. Once take up weapons as a badge of civilisation and civilisation itself is destroyed.'

'You are right, Yaghus,' Kigva said, placing her hand on his arm. 'Better these weapons should be destroyed than temptation be placed in the way of our people.'

Pryderi smiled.

'Yaghus has spoken with the wisdom of a *drewyth*. Men, no matter how advanced, given a toy, will always play with it.'

Dryden turned to Kigva and let his hand rest lightly on hers.

'I owe you my life, Kigva.'

The girl flushed a little.

'Then perhaps we have an equal standing now?' she answered.

'What shall we do with these?' interrupted Onnen, pointing to the dead Cynn.

'The forest has ways of clearing up man's debris,' answered Pryderi. 'Surely we must think about *An Kevryn*.'

182

Dryden drew his mind back to the problem.

'Yes. I must go on and track down this *morlader* named Conla.'

'I am with you, Yaghus,' declared the young *drewyth*.

Dryden shook his head.

'No, Pryderi. Your task is to escort your sister safely back to Kesmur at Dynas Dor. She has had adventures enough. It was I who promised the shade of the *drewyth* Mabon that I would seek out *An Kevryn* and bring it safely back to the temple of Meneghy. It is my responsibility and not yours.'

'No, Yaghus,' Kigva's voice was quiet but firm. 'Pryderi and I will come with you. When we return to Lan-Kern it will be together.'

Pryderi nodded his agreement. For a moment Dryden was about to protest but he gazed into Kigva's steady grey eyes, noticing the firm set of her jaw, and smiled.

'There are no two people in the world that I would rather have as my companions,' he said.

'We will accompany you as far as the northern coast,' Onnen said. 'But I doubt whether you will still find the *morlader* ships there. Having seized their booty, the *morlader* will have taken to the seas.'

'Then we will have to follow them,' Dryden answered.

Cador's eyes widened.

'Follow? Their ships are large and travel the oceans. They will probably have returned to their own country.'

'That's right,' agreed Pryderi. 'They will have returned to the isle of Manawydan. They say it is a barbaric island which is situated far north of Lan-Kern.'

'Manawydan?' repeated Dryden.

'Yes,' said Kigva. 'It is named after Manawydan, son of Llyr, the old god of the seas and oceans.'

'And if the *morlader* have taken *An Kevryn* to Manawydan, then you have no hope of returning it to Meneghy,' asserted Onnen.

'If that is so then we will fail only in the trying,' returned Dryden grimly. 'But we will try. Let's go.'

With Onnen and Cador leading the way, the five turned northwards, Dryden and Kigva bringing up the rear. As they pushed along the forest trail, heading for the coast of Lan-Howlek, Kigva let her swinging hand brush against Dryden's hand. And, after a moment, her slender fingers crept into Dryden's hand and stayed there.

183

Dryden gazed down at the girl and met her laughing gaze. He sighed. For the first time since the *Argo* had cast him upon the shores of Lan-Kern he felt happy and completely at ease.

Also available in Methuen paperback

PETER TREMAYNE

The Fires of Lan-Kern

Returning from a Polar trip, the British landscape that greeted the crew of the nuclear submarine carrying botanist Frank Dryden was completely devoid of life. The disorientated crew searched the coastline in vain for life – only ruins and mutated animals remained. Then the overworked nuclear drive exploded, leaving Dryden alone on the forbidding Cornish Peninsula. Forced to survive in an alien landscape, Dryden was befriended by the Celtic tribe of Lan-Howlek. Soon he was drawn in to their bloody battle with the evil followers of the witch, Nelferch, and underwent the painful and terrifying initiation rites of a Druidic healer. In the once and future land of Lan-Kern, Dryden began his search for the holy relic, An Kevryn – the secret key to the Universe . . .